"So he's [...]"

"Who is?" C[...] her chair in her [...]

"George Thompson."

Christal hadn't met the *St. Paul Dispatch*'s publisher, but she had certainly heard his name.

Dr. Bering looked at them all over the top of his half-rimmed glasses. "It's not totally official yet. Thompson and others are organizing a committee that will meet soon—November 2nd to be exact—and things will get started. He's got big plans for St. Paul."

Aunt Ruth tsked. "Why on earth, though? What would have possessed such a normally intelligent man to do such a thing?"

Dr. Bering chuckled. "Rumor has it that he was prompted by a certain cheeky New York journalist who declared St. Paul uninhabitable during the winter months."

Christal hugged herself happily. This was wonderful news! An ice carnival! What could it be? Her mind spun with the possibilities, all painted with the bright illustrations of the books she'd read.

"But there's more. My nephew is coming to live with me."

In first grade, **JANET SPAETH** was asked to write a summary of a story about a family making maple syrup. She wrote all during class, through morning recess, lunch, and afternoon recess, and asked to stay after school. When the teacher pointed out that a summary was supposed to be shorter than the original story, Janet explained that she didn't feel the readers knew the characters well enough, so she was expanding on what was in the first-grade reader. Thus a writer was born. She lives in the Midwest and loves to travel, but to her, the happiest word in the English language is *home*.

Books by Janet Spaeth

HEARTSONG PRESENTS
HP458—Candy Cane Calaboose
HP522—Angel's Roost
HP679—Rose Kelly
HP848—Remembrance
HP872—Kind-Hearted Woman

The Ice Carnival

Janet Spaeth

Heartsong Presents

To Higher Ground at Sharon Lutheran Church: His heart stopped, my heart broke, but your hearts were big enough for both of us. Thank you for being there when I needed you so much.

A note from the Author:
I love to hear from my readers! You may correspond with me by writing:

Janet Spaeth
Author Relations
PO Box 721
Uhrichsville, OH 44683

ISBN 978-1-60260-708-8

THE ICE CARNIVAL

All scripture quotations are taken from the King James Version of the Bible.

All of the characters and events in this book are fictitious. Any resemblance to actual persons, living or dead, or to actual events is purely coincidental.

Our mission is to publish and distribute inspirational products offering exceptional value and biblical encouragement to the masses.

PRINTED IN THE U.S.A.

one

Colorful leaves blew around Christal Everett's feet in an autumn rainbow of russet and gold. A sudden gust of air shook the trees above her, and more leaves cascaded down over her head, a veritable storm of October-painted maple and oak.

This was her favorite time of year. The world seemed so alive, almost as if celebrating a last hurrah before the long, quiet sleep of a Minnesota winter laid its white blanket over the city.

The temperature had already dropped today. What had started as a nice, sunny fall day had turned colder, with a touch of winter-to-come in the wind that had begun to pick up.

She tightened her shawl around her. Silly of her to have left the house with such a light wrap, but the morning had been sun-kissed and warm.

The days were getting shorter, and she hurried her steps homeward as shadows darkened and stretched around her. Bit by bit the wonderful houses on Summit Avenue came alive with light from inside. Just around the corner was her home. She knew that by the time she got there, her mother would have a kettle of tea ready and welcoming words to warm her heart.

Christal turned at the milliner's shop and squinted through the gathering wind toward her home. She'd dallied long enough as it was at the library, and it was time to get to work preparing dinner. Her mother had undoubtedly already started the roast.

She hurried along, her feet stirring the multicolored leaves that swirled around her shoes on the pavement. Being late seemed to be unavoidable with her, but there were so many wonderful books in the library, each one inviting her to explore its contents.

As she opened the door of her house, her mother's cheerful voice called to her. "At the library again, I presume?"

"Guilty!" Christal draped her shawl over the peg in the entryway and rubbed her hands together as she followed the delicious aroma emanating from the kitchen. "Something smells wonderful in here. What can I do?"

Mother handed her a cutting board with a loaf of freshly baked bread on it. "Why don't you cut this into slices while I finish setting the table. Did you hear that Dr. Bering is joining us later this evening?"

"I didn't know, but I'm glad. Maybe he'll play the piano for us!"

Alfred Bering had lived next door to them since they'd come to St. Paul. He was a mountain of a man, both literally and figuratively. He stood over six feet tall, and his love of cakes and breads had contributed to his substantial girth.

Yet he was a gentle giant. Hands the size of dinner plates had soothed the sick and cradled the newborn, and people came to him from all around St. Paul. He turned no one away, citing the Lord's Prayer: "Forgive us our debts as we forgive our debtors." Once he had explained to Christal that not all debts were monetary, that we all owed each other something. He often claimed that in some manner or another, everyone paid him back in the Lord's way.

The Everett family's friendship with him was born of an

early need and solidified with deep gratitude. He had been the one to see Christal through a bout with scarlet fever when she was ten and the continuing despair of rheumatic fever that had weakened her heart and kept her indoors, away from others her age.

Visits to church on Sunday mornings had been her sole outings, and books had become her friends, replacing those childhood acquaintances who had moved or drifted from her when she was ill. Dr. Bering's encouragement of a walking routine to strengthen her heart had brought her back to health.

Her parents, especially her mother, still coddled her protectively. It wasn't necessary, but it was easy to let them take care of her every need.

The sound of her father at the door drove away the remainder of her musings. "Papa!"

"None other!" Her father entered the kitchen and kissed his wife and then his daughter. "How did my lovelies spend their day?"

Christal's parents smiled at each other. It was clear that even after all these years, the two were madly in love with each other. She could see it in the way they looked at each other, their gazes locking and holding just a moment longer than with other people.

That was the kind of love she wanted. Someday she would meet a man who would look at her the same way her father looked at her mother, but so far, aside from a few tentative looks from young men in the congregation, nothing had come her way.

She sighed. Today she'd read a new book at the library. It was a children's book, but she'd been drawn by the gilded illustrations. The collection of fairy tales had taken her away from Minnesota and transported her to the land of imagination, where she had spent her afternoon.

They were charming little stories, but the fact was she lived in St. Paul, Minnesota, and there weren't princes and castles, not here anyway.

"That bread isn't going to slice itself," her mother said, laughing as she took the cutting board from Christal, the loaf still intact. "Dreaming is good, but wait until after dinner, please!"

"I'm sorry," Christal began. "I was just thinking about—"

"Hello, my dearest ones!" The grand pronouncement from the door interrupted her apology. Aunt Ruth swept in, her cerise-colored velvet dress reflecting the vivid hues of the trees outside the dining room window. Her deep black hair was piled high in a mass of curls, and elaborate earrings of garnet and pearls swung from her earlobes.

Aunt Ruth had her own apartment in the rambling house. It had been designed as maid quarters originally, but the Everetts had no maid. When Christal had become so terribly ill with rheumatic fever, Aunt Ruth had joined the Everett household to help out. She stayed, and for several years now they'd enjoyed her often-quirky style.

Christal helped her mother set out the dinner as Aunt Ruth and Papa discussed the weather, some events in the news, and preparations for a church gathering. "Dr. Bering is paying us a visit after dinner," Mother said as she seated herself. "You'll stay?"

Aunt Ruth patted the back of her flawlessly coiffed head. "Why, yes, I believe I will."

Papa smiled. "That's good. You are looking especially lovely, by the way."

Aunt Ruth sat straighter in her chair. "I believe it's time for you to ask the blessing, Matthew. Shall we bow our heads?"

Dinner sped by, as it always did, and Christal had just finished washing the last dish when she heard the awaited knock on the door. She wiped the plate, put it in the cupboard, and ran to the hallway.

Dr. Bering entered, accompanied by some windblown leaves, and she took his coat. "You'll play the piano, I hope," she said.

He laughed, a big rolling sound that poured from his round stomach. "Give my hands a chance to warm up, dear Christal. It's getting quite brisk out there. Winter is definitely on its way."

She hung his coat on the large wooden coatrack. It smelled of the smoke from many fireplaces, a sure sign of the deepening of fall.

He put his arm around her in a friendly embrace. "You could learn to play the piano yourself," he said. "There are many qualified teachers in the area. I would volunteer, but I'm not sure how I do it, so I certainly couldn't teach someone else."

"I've tried. You know that. But I just can't seem to learn it."

"Girl, you don't give yourself a chance. You need to practice every day. You can't play the piano until, well, until you actually play the piano."

She nodded. What he said was true, but the fact was that she didn't want to learn it at all. She wanted to be able to play the piano, to put her hands on the keys and have the wonderfully complex melodies flow forth just as they did when he played. She had no patience with the process of learning how to do it.

"Ruth!" Dr. Bering stopped and took Aunt Ruth's hand, raising it but stopping just short of kissing it. *Ever the gentleman,* Christal thought.

They sat in the parlor, sipping cups of black tea. Even through the everyday chitchat that surrounded her, Christal could feel something momentous was about to occur. But from whom? And what would it be?

Finally Dr. Bering set his teacup aside. It looked like a child's toy in his beefy hands. He cleared his throat and laced his fingers together across his vest and announced, "I have heard the most amazing news. St. Paul is going to have an ice carnival."

"An ice carnival? Here?" her mother asked.

"Yes, indeed. It's being planned for the first day of the new year."

"Are they daft?" Aunt Ruth frowned. "That's the worst time possible! Everyone will freeze to death!"

Papa nodded thoughtfully. "So he's really going through with it, is he?"

"Who is?" Christal leaned forward, nearly toppling out of her chair in her excitement. *An ice carnival!*

"George Thompson."

Christal hadn't met the *St. Paul Dispatch*'s publisher, but she had certainly heard his name.

Dr. Bering looked at them all over the top of his half-rimmed glasses. "It's not totally official yet. Thompson and others are organizing a committee that will meet soon—November second to be exact—and things will get started. He's got big plans for St. Paul."

Aunt Ruth tsked. "Why on earth, though? What would have possessed such a normally intelligent man to do such a thing?"

Dr. Bering chuckled. "Rumor has it that he was prompted by a certain cheeky New York journalist who declared St. Paul uninhabitable during the winter months."

Christal hugged herself happily. This was wonderful news! An ice carnival! What could it be? Her mind spun with the possibilities, all painted with the bright illustrations of the books she'd read.

"But there's more. My nephew is coming to live with me."

Only the sound of the grandfather clock penetrated the silence that followed his announcement. Then everyone spoke at once, flinging out question after question until Dr. Bering finally held up his hand.

"Wait! Here are the details. His name is Isaac. I'm importing him from Florida, to put some muscle on those arms and to thicken up that thin southern blood. By the time he's spent a winter up north, he'll be in fine shape. He'll live with me, at least until he gets situated."

"That's wonderful!" Mrs. Everett said.

"He's doing the last parts of his medical studies here," Dr. Bering continued. "When he's ready, he can join my practice."

"What's he like?" Christal asked. "Does he enjoy books?"

The corpulent physician laughed. "Right now he's spending his time poring over medical tomes, but yes, he likes to read. You'll get along well with him, Christal. He's a bit shy, so he'll benefit from your joyous approach to life."

"His faith?" her father asked. "Of course, I'm interested in that."

Dr. Bering nodded vigorously. "He loves the Lord. He was raised with that. You'll find him a stalwart member of the congregation, Matthew. Now, might I play the piano for you? How about Beethoven's 'Für Elise'?"

Christal closed her eyes as the melodic notes flowed from Dr. Bering's fingertips. Life was always good, but now it seemed to be getting even better. An ice carnival. A new friend. And Beethoven.

❧

Isaac Bering stood on the platform of the St. Paul train station and gazed around him. The trees were in full array, and the ground was strewn with shed leaves of vivid crimsons and golds, a regal array for the earth. It was stunning.

He shivered as wind whirled around his ears and leaves scrabbled across his feet. His uncle had warned him about the weather, and Isaac was, indeed, wearing his thickest coat, but the autumn air had a chill in it that told him he'd need something much more—and soon.

What had he gotten himself into? Momentary panic overtook him. He could have—should have—stayed in the safety of Florida, where the winds were warm and leaves, for the most part, stayed on the trees. Except for his uncle, he knew no one here, and even at that, Uncle Alfred was somewhat of an unknown. They knew each other primarily through correspondence. He wasn't even sure he'd recognize him.

But when Uncle Alfred had offered his home, and even more, to bring Isaac into his practice, he'd jumped at the chance eagerly. He could adapt to Minnesota. Others lived here and prospered.

He'd spent most of his life in the South, in medical school in Tallahassee and growing up in Key West, but he was up to the challenge of trying life in the North. He'd give it the best chance possible.

He straightened his backbone and stood straighter, and promptly raised his collar as the chilly wind poked icy tendrils down his neck.

A good heavy coat, a pair of fleecy gloves, sturdy overshoes, a woolly hat and muffler, and he'd be set. He could deal with a little cold.

"Isaac!"

He recognized his uncle, who hadn't changed much in the years since they'd seen each other. Uncle Alfred wrapped him in a bear hug, burying Isaac's face in the front of his jacket, which smelled of leather and wood smoke.

"It's good to see you," his uncle boomed. "Let's get your trunks and take you to the house so we can start to get you settled. How was your trip?"

Isaac couldn't stop looking at his surroundings. Never had he thought that St. Paul would be this much of a city. It was tucked away in the frozen north, after all. But St. Paul was big—bigger actually than anything he'd seen, except Chicago.

People bustled around him in an unceasing stream of humanity, like ants in an oversized anthill. Everyone seemed so busy and so sure of where they were going. If only he had their confidence.

Uncle Alfred's steady stream of words flowed over him in a meaningless cascade. If he could have slept on the train, he might be able to make sense of this, but the back-and-forth sway and the constant *ricketa-ricketa* of the wheels on the track, which had lulled his fellow passengers to sleep, had only served to keep him awake. He'd had mere sporadic snatches of sleep for the entire trip.

And he was cold.

"Are you all right, son?" His uncle looked at him in concern. "You look downright blue. Are you warm enough?"

Isaac nodded, clutching his arms to his chest in a feeble attempt at sustaining what bodily warmth he had. "Most of these people," he said, motioning to the pedestrians beside them, "are wearing only the lightest jackets. How do they do it?"

Uncle Alfred smiled. "I'm not going to give you the usual Minnesota patter about how it builds character, although I suspect it might, but the fact is that we're used to it. For us, this is simply a late autumn day. It will snow soon, maybe even next week, but to be honest with you, we tend to draw out the last moments of the waning season."

"People keep their houses warm, though, don't they?"

His uncle laughed. "Absolutely. We'll get you back to the house and put a cup of hot tea in your hands, and you'll feel better. Let's get going."

Uncle Alfred had hired a man to drive them and help with Isaac's baggage. Although, as he mentioned to Isaac, he did have his own carriage at the house. Soon Isaac was in the back of the wagon with his uncle. As they drove through the city, his uncle pointed out buildings and streets and occasionally waved at people on the streets, but it was a blur to Isaac, a big frozen blur.

Again, doubt assailed him. Had he done the right thing?

He'd taken it as his personal crusade since starting medical school to build the strength he'd need to be a good doctor. He'd been studying his Bible nightly, drawing from the powerful words of the Lord. One verse from Philippians had become his personal motto, and he repeated it at bedtime and each morning: "I can do all things through Christ which strengtheneth me."

Soon they were seated in Uncle Alfred's home, and, true to his word, his uncle had placed a large cup of black tea in Isaac's hands. He sat down across from his nephew and smiled.

"Excuse me if I study you for just a moment. I've been waiting for this, you see. Ever since your father told me that you were doing well at your medical studies but that you needed some practical experience, I prayed for this to come to pass." His uncle's voice was gentle, and in that moment,

Isaac understood why the doctor was so loved by his patients. "If you decide it's not right for you, please come to me. Let's talk about it."

"Thank you, Uncle." Isaac took a swallow of the tea and promptly choked as the hot liquid scalded his throat.

Uncle Alfred handed him his handkerchief and chuckled. "Our air is too cold and our tea is too hot."

Whatever doubts had been attacking him before vanished like rain clouds in the afternoon sun. His uncle's good humor would make this a pleasant time indeed.

A knock on the door interrupted them, and Dr. Bering ushered in a group of people. "Isaac, I'd like you to meet some good friends of mine, the Everetts."

He rose to his feet to greet them as Uncle Alfred began the introductions. The minister and his wife, his sister, and his daughter—when she looked at him, her lips curved into a contagious smile. Her deep blue eyes were lit with happiness as she shook his hand.

Christal. That was her name. It fit her, too. She sparkled like crystal.

He became aware that his uncle was talking to him.

"Christal will show you around St. Paul. She walks everywhere, so you may end up with some blistered feet at first, but no one knows the city the way she does. You two will become great friends, I am sure."

"I'm so glad you're here," she said. Her words were simple but rang with honesty. "I'm delighted that God brought you here safely."

He realized that he was still holding her hand, and he dropped it suddenly. He opened his mouth to speak, but only a croak came out. "Er, yes."

Mentally he chided himself. Why was he acting like such

a buffoon? It wasn't as if he had never spoken to a woman before. He'd had a nice social life in Florida and attended many social functions with women.

But none of them had such intelligent and lively eyes, and none of them sported a little curl of light brown hair that had escaped a coil of braids and trailed along a slender neck.

Oh, this was not good. Not good at all.

He realized that his uncle watched him, a smile playing across his face. Maybe he was wrong.

Perhaps this was good? Very good?

two

"Please join us in the parlor," Dr. Bering said as he took Aunt Ruth's shawl from her shoulders and draped it carefully over an arm of the wire coatrack. "I've got tea ready, of course, and some spice cookies—the kind you like, Christal."

"Oh, thank you so much! They are my favorite. Isaac, have you gotten to try them yet?" she said, trying not to stare at the newcomer. He was really quite attractive. His amber-colored hair gleamed in the subdued lighting, and she almost sighed. If only her hair would be that shiny! But she was stuck with plain brown hair that wasn't straight enough to be obedient nor curly enough to style into fashionable ringlets.

He shook his head. "No, I'm sorry to say that my uncle has been guarding them, saying something about them being reserved for a young woman who liked them very much."

Papa hung his wife's cape on the wire rack as he spoke. "You are in for a rare treat, Isaac. Among the good doctor's many talents is baking."

"I don't know how much talent I have in the area," Dr. Bering said, "but I do enjoy it." He chuckled and patted his stomach. "As if anyone couldn't determine that from this girth! I've sampled too many of my culinary experiments."

"We're all standing here in this drafty hall," Aunt Ruth interjected, "but I believe you have some chairs in your parlor near the fireplace if I'm not mistaken. Alfred?" She held out her hand in an obvious directive for him to move the group into the house.

17

Christal started to follow when Isaac put his hand on her arm.

"Would you like for me to take your wrap?" he asked.

She'd forgotten that she still had on her old plaid jacket. She'd put it on at Aunt Ruth's bidding. The older woman had insisted that the evening chill in the air would climb into Christal's bones and give her consumption.

There was no point in arguing with Aunt Ruth by reminding her that the two houses were next door to each other, and Christal certainly wasn't going to tell her that she often ran between the two houses in the dead of winter with no coat at all. She'd thrown on the first thing that she touched in the closet—a red and green woolen jacket that was missing more buttons than it had kept. It was a disreputable bit of clothing, and she should have thrown it away long ago. As it was, she wore it when clearing the steps of snow or helping her father clean the gutters on the roof in the fall.

And now, meeting Isaac for the first time, she was wearing it.

He must think she was the silliest goose on the planet. Or the most poorly dressed one.

Knowing she was blushing, she ducked her head and quickly attended to removing the jacket. Then she realized that bad could indeed get worse. She had misbuttoned the jacket, too, so that it was crooked and poked out at an odd angle right above her waist.

She mutely handed the offending piece of clothing to him, and as she raised her eyes, she saw laughter dancing in his taffy-colored eyes.

"I was in a bit of a hurry," she said under her breath, and he laughed.

"I see that." He hung the jacket on the coatrack with the other garments and turned to her. "Cookies await. Shall we?"

He offered her his arm, and she took it, grateful that the awkward moment had passed.

As they entered the parlor, arm in arm, conversation stopped. Her parents, sitting together on the blue velvet divan, simply smiled, as did Dr. Bering, who was in a wing chair by the side of the fireplace.

Aunt Ruth, perched on the edge of a straight-backed chair, looked like a crimson-garbed queen about to hold court. She looked pointedly at their linked arms, and her back stiffened.

She moved as if to speak, and Christal froze. Her aunt often said the most outrageous things. Isaac had just gotten here, and he didn't know how she truly spoke her mind. *Please, God, don't let her. Not here, not now.*

And then Aunt Ruth shut her mouth, leaving the words unspoken.

Christal breathed a quiet sigh of relief and said a silent prayer of thanks to God for tempering the woman's words.

She had no idea what her aunt had considered saying. The elderly woman had a strong sense of propriety, so it might have been that she thought the action inappropriate, but the truth was that Aunt Ruth was liable to say anything. However, as spontaneous as she might be, she was never intentionally mean.

"We saved your seat," Dr. Bering said in his booming voice, indicating the padded rocking chair beside the piano. "And if Matthew will pass the platter your way, you can indulge in some spice cookies."

She curled into the familiar shape of her favorite chair and took the plate of cookies her father handed over to her. The aroma was heavenly, soft cinnamon and sharp nutmeg mingled together. She took two and gave the rest to Isaac, who had taken a seat on the hassock near the rocking chair.

"Try these."

He took a bite and smiled. "They're tremendous. Uncle, will you teach me to make these while I'm here? My skills in the kitchen are limited to scrambled eggs and chops, neither of which I do well."

"Good luck. I've tried to get this recipe from him forever, and he refuses to share. You'll never get it from him, and neither will I."

Dr. Bering waved his finger chidingly at Christal. "My dear child, never say, 'Never.' Remember that the prize worth winning must be won."

Isaac leaned back and nodded. "I like that. *The prize worth winning must be won.*"

"So someday you will give me the recipe?" she asked eagerly.

Aunt Ruth cleared her throat. "It might help, child," she said, "if you could learn to light the stove."

Christal laughed. "Perhaps." Her aunt's words were true—Christal always needed help with the stove—but they stung nevertheless, and she made a mental note to work on learning it once she got home. It couldn't be that difficult. Why hadn't she ever learned how to do it properly?

Her mother intervened smoothly. "Isaac, please tell us about your family. We know that Dr. Bering is your uncle, but do you have family still in Florida?"

"Yes, ma'am." Isaac clasped his hands together, his fingers lacing and unlacing, as if he was uncomfortable with the attention. "My parents and my two sisters live in Key West. My older brother has relocated to Tennessee. He is married and has one child, a boy."

"My brother Walter is Isaac's father," Dr. Bering added. He beamed proudly at the young man.

"What drew you to medicine, Isaac?" Papa asked. "Is your father a physician, too?"

Isaac shook his head. "My father is a pharmacist."

"Now there's an interesting career," her father commented. "All those powders and potions and pills."

Aunt Ruth nodded approvingly. "I have my own remedies that suit me just fine for the most part, although I do like a drop or two of camphor when needed."

"Camphor can be very helpful, I believe," Isaac said. "My father often supplies it for deep chest congestion. It's quite effective."

"It sounds like there's a tendency toward the medical field in your family," Mother said. "Dr. Bering, was your father also interested in that sort of thing?"

Dr. Bering shook his head. "Not at all. He was a farrier and for a while had a small stable business that specialized in workhorses that businesses could use in construction. He certainly knew how to care for a horse, though, so perhaps he simply directed his mind toward horses while we focused on people."

"Did you see to the horses, too?" Christal asked. She could picture this gentle giant tending a dray horse. His large hands could easily shoe their oversized hooves.

"I did. Even young Isaac got the chance to try it. Do you remember, Isaac?"

Isaac nodded. "I do recall some of it. They were the biggest horses I had ever seen. Their hooves were the size of me, or so I thought, and I was terrified they'd step on me. And worse, they wouldn't know it. They'd just keep on walking."

His uncle laughed. "Well, they were big and you were

small. That's the truth."

"Did you get over your fear of those horses?" Christal ate the last of the spice cookies she had in her hand. This was one of her favorite moments, when the stories were told.

"I don't know that I was afraid of them as much as I was respectful of their gigantic feet. They are beautiful animals."

"What happened to the horses, Dr. Bering?" she asked.

"When my father retired, he could have sold them, but each one was precious to him, so he moved them all to his farm and let them stay until, one by one, they passed on to the Lord's pasture."

She nodded. Every good story needed a good ending, and this was a good ending.

She had many more questions, but she saw Isaac stifling a yawn. Her mother must have seen it, too, for she put her teacup on the side table and said, "This has been wonderful, but we really need to go back home. Tomorrow is Sunday, and the Lord's Day is a working day for the pastor's family, you know."

As they stood and then gathered their things from the coatrack, Dr. Bering put two more spice cookies, wrapped in a linen napkin, into Christal's hand. "I won't give you more, because I want you to come back tomorrow and take Isaac for a tour of the area after church."

She looked over at Isaac, who had taken the wretched plaid coat from the rack and now held it for her to slip into. "I'd be delighted to."

"Wear your most comfortable shoes," her father advised Isaac. "She knows every nook and cranny in the neighborhood and will probably try to show you all of them."

"I'm looking forward to that." He smiled, but she could see the lines of exhaustion around his eyes. He must be quite tired from his travels.

Christal slipped the napkin-wrapped bundle into her jacket pocket. "We'll walk through this neighborhood tomorrow. Nothing too strenuous."

"Make sure you dress warmly," Aunt Ruth interjected. "Even if you are a doctor in training, you should be careful with your own health. Bundle up."

"Oh, I will," he promised. "I am still used to the warm Floridian weather."

Aunt Ruth's blackberry-dark eyes turned toward Christal. "You, too, Christal. Just because you're a Minnesotan doesn't mean you can't catch a chill. Button that jacket."

And do it right, Christal added mentally as she took care to match the button to the buttonhole. One button hung only by a thread, and as soon as she slid it into the hole, it sprang free, clattered across the glossy wooden floor, and came to rest against Isaac's foot.

Isaac bent over and picked it up. "I believe this is yours," he said, smiling as he handed it to her.

"Thank you," she muttered, her head down. *Could this get any worse?*

Her mother moved toward the door. "Dr. Bering, it's been a lovely evening. Thank you so much for the cookies and tea. Isaac, I am delighted to meet you, and I'm looking forward to getting to know you better."

Mother took Aunt Ruth's elbow and guided her out of the house, murmuring something to the older woman as they walked through the door.

"All I said," Aunt Ruth continued as they left the house, "was that she needed a coat. Why, look at tonight. If I hadn't said something, she would have left the house without anything on her arms. It's a good thing that I—"

Her aunt's voice fading into the October night, Christal

made a promise to herself. First item of business when she got home: to shove the jacket into the ash can.

&.

Isaac hummed as he joined his uncle for breakfast. He felt like a new man, refreshed and revitalized.

"You certainly sound chipper today," Uncle Alfred boomed.

"It's amazing how much good a solid night's sleep can do," Isaac said. "No wonder so many doctors recommend it."

His uncle chuckled. "Traveling, even though one does it all by sitting down nowadays, is oddly wearing, isn't it?"

"It is." Isaac spread jam across his toast. "By the way, I'm sorry about falling asleep so quickly after our guests left last night. I wanted to help you with the dishes, but I didn't make it that far."

"You were more asleep than awake as you climbed the stairs. I don't think my china would have fared well in your hands. Bacon or sausage, or both?"

"Bacon, please."

"Eggs are ready, too. Coffee or tea?"

"Coffee, but let me get it myself. You need to sit down and eat, too." Isaac pushed back his chair and began to stand, but his uncle motioned him to sit again.

"I've already eaten. I should warn you that I'm up every day as soon as the sun comes up." He reached for the coffeepot from the top of the stove; and after wrapping the handle with a thick green cloth, he poured a cup and handed it to Isaac. "I've always been an early riser. My mother used to say that I was part rooster."

Isaac laughed.

"She, however, was like a cat," his uncle went on. "She loved to sleep, so we made a deal. I wouldn't crow when I woke up. What that meant was that I learned early on to make my own breakfast, and if there's one lesson that's served me well all these years, that's it. A man who can make breakfast on his own starts every day with an advantage."

"Why is that?" Isaac asked.

"The man who heads off into his work without food in his stomach is hobbled. Food is our fuel. You know what your books taught you. The alimentary canal is meant to have food in it to provide energy, just as a fireplace must have wood to provide heat." He patted his rounded stomach. "Perhaps it shouldn't have as much as I put in mine, however. I guess sometimes I take my own advice too much."

"It must be difficult," Isaac commented as he dug into the eggs his uncle handed him, "with food as delicious as this."

"I like to cook, as you can see. By the way, we'll walk to church this morning. It's a grand Sunday morning. The sun is shining, and the air is crisp and bright."

" 'Crisp and bright'?" Isaac repeated. "Is that Minnesotan for 'cold'?"

Uncle Alfred grinned. "You learn fast, son. You learn fast."

Isaac ate the rest of his meal quickly and dashed upstairs to finish his preparations for going to church. As he straightened his tie using the mirror over the bureau in his room, he sighed. Right on the crown of his head, a lock of hair was twisted straight up into the air.

"I look like I have a handle on top of my head," he said as he tried to comb it into place. It sprang right back up. He wet the wayward section. It didn't help.

"We need to leave," his uncle called up the stairs.

Isaac had no choice except to let his hair go its rebellious way. He hoped that by the time he got to church it would have softened, or perhaps in church it would repent and return to lying flat.

When he got to the bottom of the stairs, his uncle patted him on the back. "We need to get going. You have a real treat ahead of you. Rev. Everett is a splendid preacher, very learned and precise yet very moving. We've been lucky to have him here all this time."

Isaac reached for his overcoat, and Uncle Alfred shook his head. "It's not that cold. You don't need it."

Isaac returned the coat to the rack. Somehow he wasn't at all reassured by Uncle Alfred's words.

His uncle smiled. "You'll be fine, but you are simply going to have to develop warmer blood, Isaac. That," he said as he put on his hat and turned to look at his nephew, "and the ability not to sleep with your hair kinked under your head. Wait here."

The doctor walked quickly to his room and returned with a bottle. "This is just a little pomade, and I apologize for the smell."

Before Isaac could protest, his uncle opened the bottle, swiped his fingertips across the top of it, and ran the stuff through Isaac's hair.

The scent of lilacs and roses was immediate, almost overpowering in its intensity. Isaac coughed and waved his hand in front of his nose trying desperately to stop the odor.

"Don't worry," Uncle Alfred said cheerfully as he pulled Isaac out the door. "By the time we get to church, it should have worn off."

" 'Should'? You mean there's no guarantee?"

"You know there are no guarantees on anything except death."

"Which might come sooner than expected if I have to keep inhaling this."

His uncle was right. The day was sunny. But once outside

he had to keep himself from going back inside for his outer coat, knowing that they were late as it was. Perhaps if he walked quickly enough, he could generate enough body heat to keep himself from freezing to death before they got to church, which would—which *should*, he corrected his own thoughts—be heated.

This was a fine way to start the day, heading to worship stinking of flowers and worrying that despite it all, the recalcitrant lock would break free and point upward like a spire atop his head, perhaps reminding the other congregants that their ultimate destination lay heavenward. Plus, the small fact that he was so cold he couldn't feel his fingertips didn't help a bit.

Christal is going to be there, too, a little voice reminded him silently.

Oh, he was well aware that she would be there. She'd probably smell him before he got there, and then he'd be standing in all his wild-hair glory, his nose as red as a radish—it was too dreadful to imagine.

"Are you all right?" his uncle called, and Isaac realized he'd lagged behind. For a man as corpulent as he was, Uncle Alfred could certainly trot along at a steady pace.

Good. He'd arrive at church unable to speak, too, because he'd be so out of breath he'd be gasping for air.

This was getting worse.

He hunched his shoulders up. Perhaps that would warm his ears. He jammed his hands into his pockets and tightened them into fists, trying to expose as little flesh as possible to the cold.

How on earth did people manage this?

His uncle strode ahead—no overcoat, no muffler, no gloves, just his suit and hat. These people were insane. And winter was coming, when it would be even colder?

"Right here," his uncle called as he waited for Isaac to catch up to him. "This is the church."

Redeemer Church was built of grayish white stone with a sharply pointed steeple that rose into the sky.

Isaac leaned against the wrought iron railing and panted as he tried to regain his breath. "I must be terribly out of shape, Uncle Alfred."

Uncle Alfred clapped him on the back. "It was all uphill. On the way back, it's all downhill. Good metaphor for a church, wouldn't you say? Come in heavy laden and leave burdenless."

"That's good, Uncle. Let's go inside. I need to defrost."

His uncle smiled and shook his head. "You'll be one of us sooner than you think, Isaac."

"Is that a promise. . .or a threat?"

Uncle Alfred laughed. "Perhaps both."

Rev. Everett met them at the sanctuary door. "Welcome to both of you! Dr. Bering, you're looking well this morning. Isaac, it's good to have you with us."

The church was nearly full, and as Isaac paused to look for a spot where they could sit, his uncle whispered, "Follow me," and led him to the very front of the church to the pew where the Everetts were sitting, Aunt Ruth on the far end, Mrs. Everett in the middle, and Christal near the aisle.

There was room for only one person at the aisle end of the pew—certainly there was not enough room for someone of Uncle Alfred's girth—and the doctor murmured in Isaac's ear, "Sit here. I'll go to the other side."

The first grand notes of the processional were beginning, and the congregation stood. He slipped into the empty place and smiled as Christal held out the hymnal.

The day had just gotten considerably better. He was standing in church, singing the familiar notes of "All Hail the Power of Jesus' Name" with someone he already liked very much. He enjoyed singing in church. His ability—or, perhaps his inability—to stay on key was buoyed by the stronger voices of others, and he liked being able to blend his shaky tenor with their harmonies. The sun beamed through the rose window, the circular stained glass window behind the altar, its multicolored geometrical pattern casting rainbows of purple across the worshippers. Christal's hair was tinged violet with a section of gold in the stained light.

In the back of church, someone coughed. He didn't want to turn around to see who it was, but the sound was alarming. It had the edge of a chronic condition, and a dangerous one.

Rev. Everett began the service, and Isaac found himself listening to him with growing eagerness. The minister was engaging, just as Uncle Alfred had said.

The theme of the service was strength through the Lord. Isaac clung to every word, noting the scripture the pastor had chosen: Genesis 32:24–31. He knew the story of Jacob wrestling with God, but never before had the story come alive the way it did with Rev. Everett's sermon.

"We will close with the hymn, 'Come, O Thou Traveler Unknown,' which is based upon this story," the minister said. "As you sing the words, think of Jacob, and think of your own struggles. Whom are you struggling with? Is it yourself? With others? Or is it God Himself?"

Rev. Everett paused, letting his words sink in, and then added, "After the service, I'd like you all to meet a traveler who is *not* unknown, or at least he won't be within a few minutes." The congregation chuckled. "Isaac Bering is Alfred Bering's nephew, and he's come to continue his medical studies with his uncle. Please stop in the back of the church and greet Isaac and welcome him to St. Paul and to Redeemer."

Isaac felt himself grow warm. Having everyone in the church look at him at the same time was a very odd feeling. He managed what he hoped was a happy-to-be-here smile as he sang the words of the recessional with everyone else.

Then he saw the situation that he was facing. Sitting in the front row meant that he was the last one out, and the entire congregation seemed to be waiting for him at the end of the aisle and into the narthex.

Women in their Sunday best, men in black suits buttoned up stiffly, young girls with their hair neatly braided, and boys in miniature versions of their fathers' clothing—they all stood, anticipating something from him.

It's just this once, he told himself. *Get through this and you will not have to do it again. Think of the scripture today. Wrestle with it. Win.*

Bolstered by the morning's lesson, he cleared his throat and spoke. "I am looking forward to getting to know all of you. I'm especially grateful to have the chance to meet you first in God's house."

It must have been the right thing to say, because the women beamed in approval and the men nodded with affirmation. He shook hands and talked socially to people until at last he had met all of them, including the elderly man who continued to cough even as he welcomed Isaac.

At last, it was done. He had never done anything like that in his entire life. This was the stuff his nightmares were made of, being the center of attention and having to make conversation with this many people he didn't know.

But he had done it. And, perhaps most importantly, he had lived.

"Are we going to go for a walk this afternoon?" Christal asked as she draped her shawl over her arm.

"Christal Maria Everett!" Aunt Ruth called from across the room. "Put the shawl around your shoulders, not over your elbow."

Christal rolled her eyes but not in anger. "Aunt Ruth gets cold," she said, "so I have to put on a shawl. And a coat. And a scarf, a hat, mittens, and a muff. Overshoes. Wrap in a blanket. And then maybe I can go outside."

"I am not deaf," Aunt Ruth shot back.

"But you're chilly."

The two women looked at each other and laughed. This was a scene that the two of them clearly enjoyed, a family joke of the best kind.

"Why don't we walk home together?" Christal suggested to Isaac. "We'll go down to Summit Avenue and then back up. Is that the way you came to church?"

He hated to admit that he hadn't seen much of anything on his way to church, not while he stumbled along, hunkered over, his chin tucked into his chest and shivering the entire time.

But the sun was out, the day was warming, and Christal was good company.

They told the others of their plan and left the church.

The air had indeed lost its frosty edge, and the scene was glorious. The trees were robed in their autumn finery, and only the faintest hint of an October chill touched the light breeze.

"I love this time of year," Christal said as they walked together. She swung her shawl in front of her, and he suppressed a smile as he thought of what Aunt Ruth would have to say about that. "It's so pretty, isn't it? The earth is getting ready for winter, so God paints it as vividly as possible before all the color goes away, into the season of white, of snow and ice. What's your favorite season, Isaac?"

"I have to say that really all I've experienced is summer. Remember, I'm from Florida. Southern Florida. No snow there, so this is all new for me."

"Speaking of ice and snow," she said, stopping suddenly, "did Dr. Bering tell you about the ice carnival?"

"Ice carnival," he repeated. He shouldn't have been surprised. The people here didn't seem to know that snow and ice were cold, and that human beings were meant to be warm. Body temperature, after all, was 98.6 degrees. That was hardly compatible with living in the North.

He couldn't imagine what an ice carnival would be like. Cold, for sure.

"I don't know the details," she went on. "Dr. Bering told us about it. The man who's the publisher of the newspaper, the *St. Paul Dispatch*, is proposing it."

"Why on earth would anyone have a carnival of ice?" He shook his head. It made no sense.

She grinned at him. "Because apparently some people think it's too cold up here, that nobody could live here. Some newspaper writer said that."

"Smart fellow," he muttered under his breath.

Christal shook her head. "Give us some time. Your blood will thicken up, and you, too, will be making Aunt Ruth insane by going around in January without your coat."

"Blood thickening? Medical impossibility. Going around in January without a coat? Personal impossibility." He laughed.

"You say that now, but in the future, you'll be a tough Minnesotan, immune to the cold like the rest of us."

"Unlikely."

"Just wait. You'll see. Soon you won't be able to imagine a year without snow. By the way, how long will you stay here? Do you know?"

She swooped down and picked up a ruby and gold maple leaf and stuck it behind her ear. She looked like the picture of autumn itself.

"To be honest," he said, "I think I might stay, cold or no cold. Uncle Alfred is bringing me into his practice with the thought that eventually I'll take it over and he can retire. But of course that won't happen until I have more training and we're both comfortable with my medical skill."

"I think that would scare me," Christal said, "having someone's life in my hands."

How could he respond? Should he tell her the truth, that he was absolutely terrified of making a mistake? There couldn't be a costlier error than to make a decision that would result in death. It was irretrievable.

Would she think less of him if he spoke honestly, if he told her of his fears?

He sidestepped the issue with a noncommittal response. "That's something all physicians have to face. We try to heal, using the meager tools available to us, and sometimes, with the Lord's help, we succeed. Sometimes we don't. We do what we can, both as doctors and as human beings. The rest we commit to His power."

Christal nodded. "Your uncle is a wonderful man, as well as being an extraordinary doctor. I know he prays for his patients. He did it for me, and I really think that's what makes him so good."

"I agree. I intend to follow in his footsteps in that regard, too."

A scruffy terrier raced down the sidewalk and leaped in

joyous circles around Christal, who leaned over and cooed, "Aren't you the handsome boy? Aren't you? Yes, you are. You are a handsome boy!" Finally the dog stopped and collapsed in front of her, its belly up, until she reached down and rubbed the dog's stomach.

The dog popped back up and licked her hand.

"This is Bob," she explained to Isaac. "He's a happy dog."

"I guess so," he answered, reaching down to pat the terrier's head and being rewarded with an affectionate slurp on his palm.

"Bob will walk with us for a while, and then he'll remember that there was a squirrel he was going to chase in the tree, or he'll wonder if it's time for dinner, or maybe he'll even decide he should take a nap. But all of a sudden, he'll turn around and run back home as fast as he can."

"He sounds like quite an interesting creature." The dog leaned against Isaac's leg and gazed up at him with adoring eyes. "And very friendly."

"He is. No walk in this neighborhood would be complete without Bob. He does seem to have taken to you, though, which is quite a compliment."

"Really?" He felt oddly proud of this affirmation from the scraggly dog.

"Did you have dogs back in Florida?" she asked as they resumed their walk, Bob trotting between them.

Isaac laughed. "There are lots of dogs in Florida."

"Silly! I meant, did you have a dog?"

"When I was in school, in Tallahassee, I rented a room from a woman who wouldn't allow anything alive in the rooms—except, of course, the boarders."

"That's too bad," Christal said, as her fingertips trailed across the top of Bob's head.

"I suspect she had some pretty good reasons. I heard that too many times people had moved out and left their pets behind, and she grew tired of trying to find new homes for the animals."

"That's irresponsible—of the owners, not of her. I can understand her reasoning then. Did you have any pets when you grew up?" Christal asked.

"Any pets? Well, sure. Let's see. There were an assortment of cats and kittens that came in and out of the yard—and in and out of the house, too, much to my mother's dismay—and my father always made sure that we had a dog."

"What kind of dog?" She grinned. "Bob wants to know."

"Labrador retrievers. One of Father's favorite things is to go to the shore with his dog and throw a stick into the ocean and let the dog get it. He says there's little in life as beautiful as a soaking wet Lab proudly trotting back with the stick. He says the dog almost smiles." Isaac thought back to the blissful expression the dog had when running out of the water. "Maybe it does."

"Labrador retrievers like water," Christal said.

"You've had them, too?"

She shook her head. "No. The house belongs to the church, and as much as I'd like to have a pet of some kind, it's out of the question. When I was little, though, I would smuggle in whatever I could that would fit in my pocket. I had caterpillars and black beetles and fireflies, and once I found a toad, but I lost him somewhere in the pantry."

He burst out laughing. "The pantry! You lost a toad in the pantry? Your parents must have been quite put out with you."

"They would have—if I'd told them about it."

"You didn't tell them?"

She looked at him, her dark blue eyes wide open and

guileless, and he had a flash vision of what she must have looked like as a child. "I didn't have to. My mother found it."

"What did she do?"

"She put it back outside and then sat me down and explained that not all animals are meant to be pets, that God had them born outside because that was where they were supposed to spend their lives, and that I wasn't being kind to them bringing them inside. She said it was like putting them in prison."

"And—?" he prompted.

"And I thought she was wrong, and I told her so."

He was fascinated. "How old were you?"

"Four or five."

"What did she say when you said she was wrong?"

Christal's eyes lit impishly. "She didn't say much, because I had irrefutable logic—or so I thought."

"And your logic was—?"

"I said that Jesus had been born in a stable, which wasn't a house for people, yet he got to come inside. Nobody made him stay in the stable."

He shook his head. "How did she respond?"

"She told me that kings are comfortable anywhere, but toads aren't." Christal shrugged. "It made perfect sense to me."

He liked her family even more, just hearing her talk about them.

"How do you like St. Paul so far?" she asked. "We have toads here, just in case you want one now that I've told you my story, but they're pretty much hidden away until summer."

"Thank you, but I'll pass on the toads. Even next summer they can stay outside. I agree with your mother on that. I have to say that I have never had the faintest inclination to try to make a pet of a toad. St. Paul, though, is very beautiful.

I do believe that I chose a splendid time of year to be introduced to the city. The trees are lovelier than I could ever have imagined."

"Autumn is my favorite season, or at least it is right now," she said. "Ask me in the winter or the spring or the summer, and I might have a different answer. That's one aspect of living here that I really like: All seasons are so beautiful that I can't imagine living elsewhere. What's Florida like?"

"Florida is warm. And very humid. There are some wild storms that come in. The winds from the ocean can create some real chaos there."

"Have you ever experienced a hurricane?"

He nodded. "It was terrifying, but we came through. The wind whipped the rain so hard that the water came down like knives, or maybe I should say it came across like knives. The wind is so fierce that the rain goes sideways. There was quite a bit of damage, but we were sheltered enough that we didn't have much cleaning up to do afterwards."

She shivered. "I've read about hurricanes. We don't have them here—obviously—but there is the danger of tornadoes and blizzards and floods. No matter where we go, there will be some challenge from nature."

"Speaking of blizzards, just how cold does it get here?"

Bob stopped suddenly, nearly tripping Christal. He licked each of their hands, turned, and charged off in the direction they'd come.

"I guess that's the end of his walk!" Isaac watched the dog head for home.

"And we're nearing the end of ours."

Christal turned down a side street, and within moments they were in front of his uncle's house.

"Thank you so much," Isaac said to her.

"We'll do more exploring later," she said to him. "I want to show you the library, for one thing. I go there every day."

"Every day? You must have all the books memorized!"

"Oh, there are so many stories in there. Some I read again and again. They're like old friends to me. There are others that are new to me, and I'm always excited to open a new book and start a tale I haven't heard before."

She stopped and looked at him.

"Like me?" he asked. "Am I a new story?"

She tilted her head and studied his face. "I suppose you are. I guess the question is: Are you an adventure story? A mystery? A saga?"

His heart tripped just a bit in his chest. "And you? Are you a new story to me?"

She didn't respond, and he thought he might have been a bit too bold for this minister's daughter.

But then her lips began to curve into a slow smile. "I guess we will both have to find out."

She touched his arm lightly and turned, and with quick, light steps, she ran to her front door, where she stopped and faced him, grinning conspiratorially. "If Aunt Ruth asks, I was wearing my shawl the whole time."

He thought he already knew what kind of book she was. She was poetry.

❧

Sunday dinner over, Christal's mother and father left on their afternoon pastoral visits, and Aunt Ruth retired to her room with her knitting and her Bible. "That," she had told Christal's parents, "is the proper way to spend the Sabbath, not out on the byways of St. Paul, trotting here and there like a midwestern Sherpa."

Her parents had merely nodded, and her father said, with a

slight twinkle in his eyes, that he thought Christal was acting in the Lord's service by befriending a newcomer and helping him acclimate to his neighborhood.

Aunt Ruth answered with a sniff, but as she left the room, Christal was sure she saw a smile on her aunt's face. "Wear your jacket," the older woman called over her shoulder. "It's not July, you know."

Christal compromised with her shawl again. If necessary, she could tie it around her waist. Her aunt—and truthfully, her mother, too—would be horrified to see her doing that, but it was simply so much easier than trying to keep it wrapped around her shoulders and over her forearms. Having it around her midsection left her hands free to pet friendly dogs or pick up colorful leaves.

Isaac was waiting in the entryway next door. From the parlor behind him came the stentorian sounds of Dr. Bering's snoring.

"Are you ready to go for a walk?" she asked.

He looked behind him and grinned. "I suppose Uncle Alfred doesn't have any plans for me this afternoon."

Christal nodded. "Dr. Bering believes in Sunday rest."

"He is putting that into practice, judging from what we're hearing." He motioned toward the parlor.

"He does like his Sunday nap. But he also encourages walking as a way to health. He's told me as much. Of course," she added, leaning toward him and speaking in a conspiratorial whisper, "that doesn't apply to him. He explained it all to me once."

"Oh, he did, did he?" Amusement lit his face.

Isaac really should smile more, she thought. When he did, the worry lines and the creases over his nose, where he'd frowned too often and too long, probably as he studied his texts, vanished.

"Your uncle told me that for older people, recuperative sleep was one of the rare pleasures in life, especially in the afternoon. But we're too young for Sunday naps, so let's go for a walk. I have more of the neighborhood to show you, and I suspect that your uncle will keep you busy for the rest of the week, so this is our only chance."

Isaac reached for his overcoat, and she almost spoke but stopped. He'd just arrived, after all.

"I know," he said, "you think it's not at all cold here. I happen to know better. It is freezing. Uncle Alfred has assured me that I'll get used to it, but I don't know if that's true."

"Well, if you're going to get used to it, now's a good time to start. It'll snow soon."

"I'll get accustomed to it in stages, if you don't mind." He put on his overcoat. "In deference to the natives, though, I'll skip the hat and muffler and gloves."

"Don't tell Aunt Ruth. She'll have your head. Then freezing to death would be the least of your concerns."

They headed out the door.

"First we'll go by the library," she announced. "I know you'll spend lots of time there. I do."

He shook his head. "I don't know, Christal. I'm here to learn and study. The reading I'll be doing may not qualify as enjoyable to you, but at the moment, it's my life."

She waved away his objection. "I can't imagine life without my stories, and the library is where they are."

He seemed unconvinced, and Christal's steps slowed. Could it be possible that her new friend didn't share her love of reading?

She realized uneasily that she was interpreting it as a character flaw on his part, and it bothered her. Certainly people were allowed to have interests other than reading. Just because she found it fascinating didn't mean he had to.

God gifted people with varying talents and gave them different pursuits to enjoy. "Are you a musician, like your uncle? He plays the piano so beautifully."

"No, I'm sorry to say that I didn't inherit the Bering musical talent. I got my mother's wooden pitch."

She tried again. "Art? Do you paint?"

"No."

"Athletics? There are some superb organizations—"

"Along with my mother's wooden pitch, I got her arms and legs. No athletics. I can't catch a ball, nor run, without tripping."

"Do you cook?" She thought of her own deficiency in that area.

"No."

"Garden?"

"No."

"Travel! You like to travel, don't you?"

He sighed. "Again, no. Christal, I am a very boring person. Boring Bering."

"You are not boring!"

"I am, I'm sorry to say. Medical students are traditionally among the worst. We have a terrible leaning to single vision. We make the worst dinner companions and often have to be stopped short of an invigorating discussion of nephritis over pound cake and coffee."

"Nephritis?"

"Kidney disease."

"Oh." She could only imagine the details of such a conversation.

"If I begin to ramble on about gout or infections of the

sinus cavities or spasms in the esophagus, you'll please bring me back to the here and now?"

She laughed. "With pleasure!"

They were nearly to the corner where the library was. It was, of course, closed on a Sunday afternoon, so all she could do was point out the brick building that housed the library on the second floor.

Perhaps it seemed odd to him that she had brought him all the way there, just to show him the exterior of the library—not that he seemed even faintly interested in it.

"There are doctors' offices on the ground level." She added the last bit with hope. Maybe at the very least that would entice him to return.

He didn't respond.

"There are all kinds of wonderful stories in there," she said, "even, I'm sure, about the history of inflamed nostrils and the philosophy of sutures."

His roar of laughter filled the almost empty street, and the few pedestrians that were out on a Sunday stopped and smiled curiously at the sound.

He reached for her hand and held it in his. "I am so sorry. I'm afraid I've offended you."

She knew she was growing flushed, partially because he had done just that, even though she had fought her reaction to his indifference, and partially because he was holding on to her hand and it felt so good.

"Philosophy of sutures, indeed. Christal, I am having an absolutely wonderful time today. Why, I'm not even cold."

His nose was red, and the tips of his ears were bright crimson. The chest of his overcoat rose and fell rapidly. The poor fellow looked wretchedly uncomfortable.

"You are cold, and I've probably worn you out," she said,

taking pity on her new friend. She touched his arm. "Let's go back. We'll walk more slowly, and the next time you can wear a hat and scarf and gloves. Truthfully, you'll probably need them by then."

"The next time," he repeated. "Until it warms up, that's as likely as my taking my own tonsils out."

Her heart sagged in disappointment, but she reminded herself again that God made all of His creatures blessed in diverse ways. He didn't *have* to like reading to be her friend, and he didn't *have* to like the cold weather as much as she did.

"You know, it could warm up again a bit," she said in what she hoped was an encouraging voice. "Indian summer usually comes earlier, like the end of September or the beginning of October, but there's nothing to say it couldn't happen now."

"Really?" he asked, his voice perked with renewed optimism.

"I think it could," she declared stoutly. "Why, even as I stand here, I can still smell the remnants of a garden, so they haven't all died."

He drew a deep breath, and his forehead puckered in confusion. "I can't smell it. Are you sure?"

"I am. Lilacs and roses. There's been a hint of them all day. So maybe summer still has one more hurrah in it."

Isaac cleared his throat and ran his hand over the top of his head. Why were his cheeks suddenly as florid as his ears and his nose? Was he really *that* cold?

Christal shrugged away the odd gesture. Southerners!

❧

Christal closed her Bible and placed it on her bedside. When she had fallen ill nearly a decade ago with scarlet fever, she'd begun her own tradition of reading the twenty-third Psalm each night before going to sleep. Of course she had it memorized, but the comfort of holding the Bible that had been hers since she was an infant was part of the ritual.

The promise of the psalm that she would walk through the threat of death, *the valley of the shadow of death*, had been soothing. The days when she had hovered between life and death were tempered by the words *I will fear no evil, for Thou art with me*. Even when she hadn't been able to talk, when she was lost in the dreams of a high fever, she had held the words closely to her heart.

She could see a glow from the upstairs window of Dr. Bering's house next door. One of the men was awake, too, reading perhaps.

The night air was sweet with the smell of fireplaces, and she padded over to the window to open it an inch or two to let the aroma in and to chase the staleness of the closed room out.

From below her came the faint notes of Beethoven's "Moonlight Sonata." Dr. Bering must be playing the piano in his parlor.

There had never been such a beautiful piece of music. She sat beside the window and rested her chin on the windowsill and let the notes float over her. It was liquid.

She closed her eyes and let her mind drift as she revisited all of the wonderful things that had happened in the course of the day. This had been an absolutely perfect day, from worshipping with Isaac and getting to know him a bit, to this serene end with "Moonlight Sonata" and smoke-scented air.

Isaac. Her thoughts paused and lingered. Isaac.

There was something very special about him. How special, she didn't know yet. Only God knew that.

Christal opened her eyes and looked again at the house next to hers. Isaac Bering was going to be a good friend—that much she knew. One should never overlook the value of a good friend.

Especially, she thought with a grin, a good friend who was as handsome as Isaac.

The October night breeze had an edge to it, and she closed the window some more, leaving it open enough to freshen the air and allow the music in.

"Good night," she said softly to the house next door. "Good night, and God bless you."

three

"There is only one door between my office and my living quarters," Uncle Alfred explained as he led Isaac through the heavy oak door that separated the entryway and the waiting room of his medical suite.

"Just one door? Why is that?" Isaac asked.

"There are several reasons for that," his uncle responded, "but the major one is simply to keep myself from spending all of my evenings in here, reading and puttering. I guess you could say it's symbolic. A doctor must keep a part of his life separate from the practice of medicine."

The waiting room was situated on the front corner of the house so that windows opened two of the walls to daylight. An opulently upholstered sofa with golden oak arms polished to a silken sheen sat along one side of the room, while wing chairs covered in burgundy brocade were positioned next to the small fireplace.

A glass-fronted bookcase held three rows of leather-bound volumes, each with the title stamped in gold. Isaac wandered over to them. Many of them he recognized from his own early school studies, but the others weren't familiar.

On a small table three volumes were placed in an inviting display near a figurine of an angel holding a child. Isaac picked them up and read the authors aloud. "Charles Dickens. John Keats. Jules Verne. This is quite the assortment here, Uncle Alfred. Are you reading these, or are they for your patients as they wait?"

"I keep them here for anyone to read. If a patient or his family happens to start reading a book and wants to continue, he's more than welcome to take it."

"Aren't you worried about losing the book?" Isaac touched the thick binding of one of the volumes. It wasn't an inexpensive edition.

"I always get them back, but even if I didn't, I wouldn't care. Books are meant to be shared."

His uncle clearly shared Christal's love of reading. It baffled Isaac. These kinds of books, with things like poetry and tales, served no educational purpose that he could see. Why else would one read, unless one wanted to increase one's knowledge? "You've read these?"

"Indeed." Uncle Alfred opened the Jules Verne volume. "Ah, *Around the World in Eighty Days*. What an intriguing story! Have you read it, Isaac?"

"No, I'm sorry, I haven't. Schooling seems to occupy almost every waking minute of my time."

His uncle shook his shaggy head. "Don't let yourself fall into that trap, my boy. A good doctor reads novels, visits with people, goes to concerts, gets out and about. The more you know, the better you'll be as a physician. People rarely act like they're shown in the textbooks. The cases in there are artificial. It's important for you to know what's going on in the world, to find out what people are really like."

He shoved the book into Isaac's hands. "Read this."

Isaac stared at the novel. "But this is fiction."

"Yes." Uncle Alfred hooked his thumbs under his suspenders and watched Isaac with a slightly bemused expression. "You don't like fiction?"

"I do, I guess." Isaac was at a loss. He hadn't read a novel in years. "Shouldn't I be reading medical texts at this stage?

After all, I'm here to learn."

"You will learn by reading novels, too, Isaac. Stretch your mind. Expand your knowledge. Learn expansively."

Jules Verne? He'd heard of Jules Verne and his novels of fantastic adventures that did not take place in the world Isaac knew. His uncle wanted him to read something by a Frenchman that was based upon a science that didn't exist? Science and fiction—now there were two terms that should never go together.

He started to put the book back onto the table, but his uncle stopped him. "I'm serious, Isaac. Read the book. Try something different."

Try something different? Wasn't he already trying something different, leaving his home in Florida and moving north, coming into a land of ice and snow that his body would take months, if not years, to get used to? He had left the rest of his family and his friends and committed himself to at least two years with an uncle he barely knew—an uncle he respected but with whom he'd spent little time.

He looked back at the books on the shelves. He was used to spending long hours poring over medical tomes filled with information that he would desperately need, and yet here he was being told to read a novel filled with crazy science.

His uncle led him through the rest of the office area, through the examination room with its assortment of tools and instruments that his uncle used in the course of the day, and on into the lab and surgery.

He took one look at the surgical bed and swallowed. This was the part he was not ready for. The dangers were so great.

Uncle Alfred must have understood his nephew's hesitation, for he rubbed Isaac's shoulder in sympathy. "I hope the day never comes, Isaac, when you walk in here and aren't overcome with the enormity of the responsibility you face. If you ever lose that and become complacent, your doctoring skills will have failed you."

Isaac leaned against the bed to steady himself. He had made a terrible mistake. He was not meant to be a doctor.

He looked at his hands, trembling and unsure. At some point, he would stand in the room and his fingers would grip a scalpel. He would be expected to cut into a patient's skin and open his body and heal him.

A mere mortal could not do that. *He* could not do that.

"You'll be fine," his uncle declared. "This self-doubt does serve a purpose, you know. It means that you will think before you act, which is imperative for a physician. You do, however, need to control it. You'll be no good if you're unconscious on the bed beside your patient. One of you has to hold the scalpel, and it really should be you."

He led Isaac out of the surgery area, through the examination room, and back to the waiting area. "My first patient will be here soon. I would like for you to join me in the evaluation of his symptoms."

Isaac put the Jules Verne volume on the table. "I promise," he said, before his uncle could object, "to take it with me when I'm through here."

"Good, because—well, hello, Mr. Lawrence." Uncle Alfred helped the patient off with his coat.

Isaac recognized the man from church the day before. His cough had punctuated the service, and yet he had stayed to meet Isaac afterward.

"So your throat is quite irritated?" Uncle Alfred led Mr. Lawrence into the examination room. "I'd better take a look at it. By the way, this is my nephew, Isaac Bering, who is going to continue in my footsteps. You might remember him from church yesterday."

"I do," the man replied, stopping for a moment as coughing wracked his body. Then he continued, "Isaac, I'm praying you enjoy your time here. Your uncle is a good man and a good doctor."

"Thank you, Mr. Lawrence. From what I've seen of the city, I'm impressed. It's beautiful. And I concur with your assessment of my uncle."

"You two will make this old doctor blush," Uncle Alfred said. "Mr. Lawrence, I hope you don't mind if Isaac joins us today."

And with those words, Isaac's journey into medicine took one step forward.

❧

"And wear your jacket!"

Aunt Ruth's words followed Christal as she left the house. The morning air still retained a bit of the night's chill, but the sun blasted away, and soon the day would warm up considerably.

She had a jacket with her—not the dreaded plaid one, though. She reminded herself again that she needed to get that horrible garment into the fire as soon as possible. This one was a sedate black short coat, the one she usually wore to church. A bit fancy, perhaps, for her errand, but it was better than the plaid jacket.

The door opened at Dr. Bering's house, and she watched Isaac steadying John Lawrence on his way down the front walk. Mr. Lawrence was coughing badly, and she immediately prayed for his health. Over the past two or three months, the elderly man had developed a deep congestion that seemed to have grown worse every time she saw him.

"Hello, Mr. Lawrence!" she called, waving at him. "Hello, Isaac!"

Isaac raised his free hand in a salute. "I'm going to go with Mr. Lawrence here to see his bird, Aristotle."

She smiled. Aristotle was a mangy-looking and terribly ill-tempered bird "of some undetermined heritage, an avian vagabond," but she suspected that the bird was a common crow.

As far as she'd been able to tell, Aristotle's sole talent was that he was in love with the image he saw in the mirror that Mr. Lawrence had put behind his cage. *Just like some people I know.* Aunt Ruth had sniffed after a visit when Aristotle had been particularly rambunctious and bitten the feather off her new hat.

Christal had wondered if perhaps the bird realized the source of the feather—one of its distant and undoubtedly deceased relatives—and had attacked the feather as a way of punishing Aunt Ruth.

The bird's place in Mr. Lawrence's heart was well known, but Dr. Bering, she was sure, hadn't sent Isaac out just to see the bird.

"Would you like to come, too?" Mr. Lawrence asked, covering his mouth as the coughing rose again.

"I'd love to see Aristotle. Let me just pop back in and tell my mother that I'm going with you two first."

She turned and went back into the house. Her mother was headed up the stairs with an armful of folded linens and stopped. "I thought you were going to the library."

"I am, but first may I go with Isaac to see Mr. Lawrence's bird? They're going now, and Mr. Lawrence invited me."

Mother shifted the sheets and frowned slightly. "You know, I think that would be a good idea. He sounds so sick lately, and I'm worried about him. Christal, without being obvious about it, will you take a look at his home and see if he might need some help? I can't think that he's able to keep up with it, not as ill as he must be."

"I will." She kissed her mother lightly on the cheek. "I'll see you later."

She rejoined the two men and walked with them to Mr. Lawrence's house. It was less than two blocks away, but the elderly man walked so slowly that it took them almost half an hour.

His house was small and sunlit. As soon as they walked into the living room, loud squawking and chirping broke the morning calm.

Aristotle hopped from one foot to the other in a kind of wild dance. Up and down the rod that crossed his cage he went, screeching and shrieking until Mr. Lawrence hobbled over to see him.

"Aristotle, are you glad to see me? Say hello to your papa! Say hello!"

Isaac looked at Christal, and they smiled as the aged man fussed over his beloved bird. He opened the door and thrust his hand inside the cage. The bird popped onto it and immediately bit his knuckle.

"Here's my boy!" Mr. Lawrence announced as he held Aristotle out to Christal and Isaac.

She tried not to smile as Isaac nodded uneasily, as if not sure if he was expected to let the bird get on him or to pet it.

The question was resolved quickly when the bird flew to the top of the bookcase with a great shower of feathers that dropped off him and drifted onto every nearby surface.

"Should I get him?" Isaac asked. The expression on his face clearly showed that he hoped the answer was no.

"He'll be fine. I let him out to stretch his wings every once in a while." Mr. Lawrence stopped as a round of coughing took over.

"My uncle has given you a bottle of medicinal syrup for that," Isaac said, reaching into his pocket. "Let's get some in you before I leave."

"I'll get a spoon," Christal said. "I know where the kitchen is."

The dishes were piled on the counter, crusted with dried food. Mr. Lawrence had apparently made some effort to clean a few of them, judging from the ones that were drying on a towel near the sink.

Her mother's fears were right. The poor man was overwhelmed with housekeeping now that he was sick.

He hadn't always been like this. Usually the house was spotless. But now dust motes as thick as June stars danced in the sunlit living room, and the bright light through the window showed where he had missed cleaning up after his bird.

Christal blinked as tears burned into her eyes. Was Mr. Lawrence going to get better? He had to! She couldn't bear seeing him like this, failing so dramatically.

As she found a clean spoon, wiping it off just in case, she remembered when she had been younger and had come to his house to see the bird and to look at his flower garden. Now both he and the bird were old, and the flower garden had gone to weeds.

She ran her fingertips over her cheeks to dry off the last vestiges of tears and practiced a smile. There. She could go back in and see him.

"I've got it!" she sang out as she joined the two men. Isaac stood beside Mr. Lawrence, comforting him as yet another set of coughs shook his frail body. The medicine was already in his hand. Even the cork was out.

"Here," he said, taking the spoon from her and pouring the syrup into it. "This will help control the spasms in your lungs, and it'll let you sleep."

Aristotle flapped his wings and shrieked from his perch on the bookcase.

"I wish I could get him back in his cage," she said to Isaac, "but I'm afraid he'd tear me apart."

"He's a good bird," Mr. Lawrence said from the chair, his voice growing slurred as the medication quickly took effect. The sedation in the syrup, combined with the effort of the walk to and from Dr. Bering's office and the wearying rounds of deep coughing had clearly exhausted him. "He'll go back in."

And with that, he put his head to one side and fell asleep.

"Well," Isaac said, "I guess that's that."

Christal took a throw from the divan and covered the older man. "I'll tell my mother. She'll come in and see to him."

They tiptoed out of the room as Aristotle made another loop around the room, coming to rest this time on the curtain rod.

Isaac shook his head. "I'm not going after that creature."

"Nor am I. We'll leave him. There's food in his cage, I noticed, so I'm sure he'll head back in there eventually."

Once they were out on the street, Isaac shook his head. "That poor man."

"He's sick, isn't he, Isaac?" She reached out and grasped the sleeve of his coat, making him stop. "Tell me, please."

"Yes, he's sick."

"Is he going to get better?" *Please say yes,* she added mentally.

He shrugged and looked away. "That's God's decision."

A sob tore at her throat. That was answer enough.

She dropped her hand from his arm and shoved it into her

coat pocket. It wasn't fair. "People should live forever. They should never get sick."

He didn't speak at first. Then, "Well, of course we live forever. Not on earth, but in heaven." He smiled wryly. "Here I am, telling a pastor's daughter about eternal life."

"I do know that, and it is a comfort, but still, that's for the person dying. They get to go on to eternal life, while we who are left here have to wait for our turn. I don't like that part."

"I know," he said softly.

"I've been to a lot of funerals as a minister's daughter. Sometimes I barely even knew the person, sometimes not at all. But sometimes I did know them well, and it hurts so badly." She sighed. "I understand it all, but I don't like seeing people hurting."

"Nor do I, Christal, nor do I." They began to walk back toward the Bering house. "That is the reason I became a doctor, to try to ease pain wherever I could."

Neither one said anything until at last Christal said, "You know, Mr. Lawrence could have walked home by himself. He's weak and he proceeds slowly, but he walks everywhere he goes. I wonder why your uncle sent you with him."

Isaac stared thoughtfully at the road ahead. "Uncle Alfred cares about his patients as people. Each one is an individual human being, and their needs extend beyond what they might tell him in the consulting room. I suspect he wanted me to see Mr. Lawrence's home and to see his relationship with that silly bird."

She looked at him curiously. "Why?"

"Because that's all part of who John Lawrence is. He's a person. Right now he's a person who has a terrible cough." He shook his head. "I don't know. I don't know what to think, except that Uncle Alfred's success as a physician is due, in part, to his ability to treat the person, not the disease."

That made sense to her. Dr. Bering had an astonishing talent to understand his patients and their needs.

They were at the foot of the walk to her house. "I'm going to go in and talk to my mother about Mr. Lawrence. I'm sure she will make sure his house is put in order—and don't worry, she'll do it in a way that he probably won't even realize it."

"Not realize it?" Isaac asked. "Be realistic, Christal. You saw it. If she cleans even a little corner of the house, it'll be noticeable."

Christal smiled. "Many years of being a good minister's wife have given her plenty of experience in being tactful with those in the congregation who are in need but don't admit it. She'll find a way to take care of it so he won't be hurt. By the way, I'm going to the library in a while. That's where I was headed originally. Would you like to join me?"

She held her breath as she awaited his answer. It was silly, wanting him to join her there, but the fact was that if she could create a perfect friend for herself, it would be someone who would love the trips to the library as much as she did.

"I can't. My uncle has patients all day long, and I need to be back there, learning at his side."

Her disappointment must have shown on her face, for he touched her hand. "I will go another time, Christal. It's important to you, so it's important to me."

It was the perfect answer. He smiled at her, his golden brown eyes meeting hers directly. The sun had risen to its midmorning glory, and his hair caught the light.

She was so glad he was here.

At last she shook herself out of her reverie. It could only have lasted a second or two, but it seemed longer. "I'll see you another time then."

He reached out and touched her arm. "Yes, indeed."

As he walked over to his uncle's house, she headed up the walkway to her own front door and marveled at how much happier he made her. Even in the midst of pending sorrow, he brought something very special into her life.

Her mother met her in the entryway as Christal was taking off her jacket. "Christal, what did you see?"

"There are dishes that need to be washed, the furniture is dusty, and the bird is loose. That's all I saw, but it's quite a lot."

Mother reached for her coat. Her ragbag was at her feet, ready for service.

"I'm going over now, then. Can you please let Aunt Ruth know? She's in the parlor with her knitting."

"I'll go with you." The library could wait. This was more important. "Let me—"

"We'll all go." Aunt Ruth's tone brooked no discussion. Christal hadn't even heard her come into the hall. "The three of us should be able to put the house to rights quickly. We need to be careful not to disturb him while we're there, so the sooner we can get done, the better."

"I think he's asleep," Christal offered. "He must have been tired anyway, and then Isaac gave him some syrup that Dr. Bering had sent. There must be some powerful medicine in it. He fell asleep almost immediately."

Her mother and aunt looked at each other and nodded. "For the cough," Mother said. "He has to sleep in order to build up his strength to battle the cough."

"Put on your jackets, both of you," Aunt Ruth ordered as they were leaving. Christal and her mother grinned at each other—and put on their jackets.

The three women trekked the short distance to Mr.

Lawrence's home, as Mother and Aunt Ruth mapped out a strategy for dealing with the situation there. Her mother listed the contents of her bag. "Rags, of course. A bar of good strong soap. That scrub brush we use on the stairs in the back. Vinegar. Ammonia."

They arrived at the Lawrence home. Mother knocked. When there was no response, she opened the door and called out softly, "John Lawrence? Mr. Lawrence? It's Sarah Everett, the minister's wife. Ruth and Christal are with me. Might we come in?"

She motioned to Aunt Ruth and Christal to follow her.

Mr. Lawrence was just as Christal and Isaac had left him only moments before, asleep in his chair. Aristotle screeched, but Aunt Ruth reached into her pocket and pulled out something that she held toward the bird.

Aristotle flapped over to her, snatched it out of her hand, and carried his prize again to the top of the bookcase.

"What on earth was that?" Christal asked, amazed.

"A slice of apple. I was knitting, and you know how much I enjoy a cut apple while I knit. It's much easier and less sticky to have it in pieces. Well, waste not, want not. I brought it with me when we came here. I know that Aristotle likes apples."

"How?" Christal couldn't keep the astonishment from her voice. "How did you know that?"

"Christal Maria Everett," her aunt admonished, "just because a woman might be old doesn't mean she's lost all her faculties. Or that she doesn't know someone. John Lawrence and I have known each other for many years, even before Aristotle came into his life. And do you know *why* Aristotle has such a spot in John's heart?"

Christal looked at the bird perched on the bookcase. His

feathers were a splotchy mixture of brown and black, and in places they appeared to be thinner than others. His beak was chipped slightly, and one eye had a film over it.

Why the creature had a spot in anyone's heart was beyond her.

"Come into the kitchen with me, child, and you and I can tackle it while your mother attends to the living room. Sarah, you might want to consider cleaning the birdcage first and putting in some fresh seed. I think Aristotle might actually fly into it by himself if it's not so messy."

Mother smiled at Christal as Aunt Ruth marched into the kitchen. "Guess I'll start with the birdcage then!"

They moved quietly so as not to awaken Mr. Lawrence or startle the bird. Aunt Ruth began the process of heating water for washing the dishes as they both worked on the general disorder of the room.

"It looks like he would get started and then quit," Aunt Ruth said. "Of course he's so sick he probably has the energy of a footstool."

"A footstool?" Christal asked with a grin.

"Don't be impertinent," Aunt Ruth said with a mischievous glint in her eyes. "By the way, do you want to hear about Aristotle?" She picked up a stack of newspapers. "We can take care of these right now. It's only called 'news' when it's new. These probably date back to the Lincoln administration."

She handed the papers to Christal who stacked them by the door. They'd leave a few for cleaning the birdcage, but most of them would be thrown out.

Aunt Ruth ran her hand over the counter. "This needs a good cleaning, too. But about the bird. John was married to a beautiful woman, and he adored her. He was older than she was, maybe fifteen years, possibly twenty. I don't remember exactly. She got sick, though, very early in the marriage, and she didn't live."

"How sad!" Christal exclaimed.

"It was. For the longest time, an aura of melancholy surrounded him. He was there, but he wasn't, if you know what I mean. His heart wasn't in anything he did."

"He must have missed her terribly."

"Oh, he did. He was a good man, but the joy left him when she died. I'm not saying that he never laughed or smiled—he did indeed—but I could tell that he seemed to have buried himself with her."

Christal sighed.

"But then one day he found Aristotle in the yard. The bird was a tiny broken thing, and most of us who knew John thought it was a bad idea for him to get attached to it. It's quite hard to raise a bird anyway, but a wild bird that's just a baby and injured, too—well, we didn't see how the thing could survive. So we discouraged John."

"Wouldn't it be a good thing?" Christal asked, starting to mop the floor. "I'd think it might take his mind off his wife's death."

"Honey, nothing can take your mind off a spouse's death. It comes and sits in you and it never, ever leaves. It's been twenty-seven years since my Theo went to his reward, and there isn't a day I don't think of him. Anyway, we thought John had put all his hope in this little bird, and we knew he'd be devastated if it died, too, but the thing survived and has lived with him ever since."

"Since it's a wild bird, wouldn't it be better if it was out-side?" Christal rinsed the mop in her bucket, and as she wrung it out, the water ran so dark it looked like mud.

She remembered her pet toad, and her counterargument

that Jesus had been born in a stable, and the explanation her mother had given her that kings can live anywhere but wild animals must live outside.

Aristotle didn't seem like a king.

"I'd think it was unkind to keep the bird inside. It should have been outdoors, where it could fly free," Christal said, leaning down to get a spot she'd missed. "I think Aristotle would be happier if he had the entire neighborhood to annoy."

"He's got something wrong with his wing," Aunt Ruth told her as she attacked the grime on the stove. "He can fly a little bit, but he would die outside. So John saved Aristotle, and I think Aristotle saved him."

Christal nodded and peeked around the corner. The bird had moved closer to her mother, who was carefully cleaning out the cage. Now that she understood why Aristotle meant so much to Mr. Lawrence, the bird didn't look quite as disreputable.

It flapped over to her mother, lit on her head, and nipped her ear. Her mother yelped softly with surprise and waved the bird away.

Christal shook her head. No matter what, the bird was cranky, even if it was beloved by Mr. Lawrence.

She and Aunt Ruth set to soaking and washing the dishes. It was quite a process, but apparently Aunt Ruth had never met a plate that she couldn't get clean. She scrubbed until it seemed the pattern might come off.

As Aunt Ruth washed and Christal dried, they talked about the weather and the preparations for Christmas that were already under way even though it was still October. Christal was used to planning for Christmas this early. That was the life of a minister's family. Having two holidays come so close together—Thanksgiving and Christmas, both of which required special services and celebrations—meant they had much to do to be ready.

A church member had proposed that the church supply a festive meal for a poor family or two at Christmas, and at the moment Papa was busily working on the details of such an arrangement.

"People don't always like to be helped," Aunt Ruth said as she handed a pan to Christal. "Here. I finally got the last bits off. I was nearly at the point of throwing it out and simply buying him a new one."

Aunt Ruth sometimes had the ability to carry at least two conversational threads at the same time. Christal had learned to wait it out if it got confusing. Her aunt would eventually resolve it.

"So we have to be careful when we choose this poor family, which is, of course, quite logical. No one wants to be categorized as 'that poor family,' especially then to become the ward of the church no less. So how do we do this without hurting their feelings? Careful, now, I believe that cup is Limoges. And it must be old. I wonder if it wasn't his wife's."

"Mother will know how to do it," Christal said. "She can do that kind of thing."

"The thing is," her aunt said as she wiped out the basin, "to be able to figure this out on your own without relying on her. You're getting old enough that you need to quit expecting her to do everything. Your mother is, without a doubt, the picture of tact, and she will have some way of making the family the church selects feel as if they've won a treasure. But what would *you* say, Christal?"

The question made Christal uneasy. She knew she didn't have her mother's diplomatic skills, and the thought of the possible missteps she could make terrified her. "I probably wouldn't say anything. Maybe, 'Here's some food.'"

Amusement flitted across Aunt Ruth's face. "And then when they asked where the food came from, what would you say?"

"I'd probably stammer out something like, 'People. It came from people.' And then I'd turn and hurry away."

"My dearest niece, you are charming, but you do lack your mother's poise, don't you? I don't think it's quite that simple. John Lawrence is snoozing away in the other room, but what happens when he wakes up and sees that three women have come into his house, uninvited, and cleaned it? What will you say?"

" 'Surprise'? Oh, I don't know. We don't want to say that his home is a mess, do we? But what *can* we say? Maybe we should just sneak out and let him wonder."

"And have him doubt his sanity? He knows what the house looked like when he fell asleep. Imagine his reaction if he wakes up and it's all cleaned."

"Like the shoemaker and the elves!" Christal thought of the fairy tale that had been her favorite when she was a child. She'd hated cleaning her bedroom, so the story of the elves who did the shoemaker's work while he slept had been quite appealing.

"I think he's a bit old for fairy tales. I wonder—"

What her aunt had been about to say was interrupted by a loud snort as John Lawrence woke up in the living room.

"Sarah Everett, what are you doing here?" he asked, his voice still slurred from sleep.

"Listen carefully," Aunt Ruth whispered in Christal's ear. "Learn from what she says."

They moved to the doorway where they could watch but

not be seen by the elderly man.

Mother straightened the blanket over his feet. "You've been sick, you know, and my Christal came by with Isaac Bering to visit with you and Aristotle. Do you remember that?"

"Yes." His voice was raspy from the extensive coughing, but the hacking had stopped.

The medicine must be working, Christal thought.

"I wanted to see if there was something you needed, but you were asleep. I hope you don't mind that I let myself in. Christal and Ruth are with me, by the way." She motioned them into the room. "We wanted to visit with you. Aristotle was out of his cage, so I thought it was the perfect opportunity to clean it out."

He nodded, but he seemed a bit confused still.

"While we were waiting, we just puttered around a bit here and there, trying to make things a bit easier for you during your recovery."

"You didn't have to."

Mother patted his hand. "Maybe not, but you can't tell me that if you put three women in a house that's lived in by a man and his bird, that those three women aren't going to be fixing things. Remember when we had that door that wouldn't close? You had stopped by for something else, and when you saw it, you got your tools and dealt with it right then and there."

"Ah, I do remember. That was a long time ago." He put his head against the back of the chair and closed his eyes.

"But I still remember it." Mother smoothed back a strand of white hair that had fallen over his forehead. "One always remembers a kindness."

A smile drifted over his lips before he succumbed again to sleep.

Mother tucked the wrap under his feet again. "Sleep well, my friend."

With those words, the three women tiptoed out of his house and back into the October brightness.

"Are you going on to the library?" Mother asked.

Christal shook her head. What she had just learned today, about giving with kindness, was too big to dilute with a light fable or tale. She looped her arms through her mother's and aunt's. "Let's go home."

❧

Isaac closed his Bible and laid it on the table in his room. He'd read through, yet again, the story in Mark of the woman who "suffered many things of many physicians" and who touched the hem of Jesus' clothing and was healed.

Jesus said to her, "Daughter, thy faith hath made thee whole; go in peace, and be whole of thy plague."

He leaned back and thought about those words. John Lawrence had the faith of many, yet he also was not young, and his body wasn't up to the fight that his illness was wreaking. Would his faith make him complete in heaven?

He knew the answer. He opened his Bible once more, but the autumn sun had diffused to twilight, and he struggled to make the words out in the dim surroundings. He could get up and light the lamp, but he wanted to sit and reflect.

Again he closed the Bible, this time holding it against his chest as he shut his eyes and thought.

This had been his first day in the practice of being a doctor. With his uncle, he had seen several patients, but John Lawrence was the one who had crawled inside his heart and stayed there. Perhaps it was because of the old friendship between his uncle and Mr. Lawrence.

Isaac knew that Uncle Alfred had sent him home with

Mr. Lawrence for a reason, but he hadn't explained. And while he was certain his uncle hadn't set it up this way, it was interesting that his first patient was a man who was heaven-bound.

He remembered something his father had told him once, that medicine wasn't completely about a physical cure but about making people comfortable on their earthly journey to their reward. Often the two were one and the same, but not always.

Isaac shook his head. He needed to think about something else. He got up, lit the lamp, and picked up the volume his uncle had given him, the Jules Verne novel. Soon he was following the adventures of Phileas Fogg as he tried to circle the world in eighty days.

His mood brightened as he read eagerly, and when finally exhaustion forced him to lay the book aside, he understood why his uncle was so insistent that he develop an outlet like recreational reading. It would serve him well in future days like this.

Isaac got into bed and pulled the blankets up to his chin, staying still until his body warmed up. From below, the calming notes of a Brahms melody floated from the piano as his uncle played before he, too, went to sleep.

It had been quite a day, and as he drifted off, thoughts of a wild bird and an old man mingled with those of a young woman who had a smile like an angel. Yes, it had been quite a day.

four

Autumn took its crimson and golden garments and left as November entered with the icy breath of winter. The first frosty flakes of snow fell, melting as they hit the still-warm earth; and then, as the days moved toward the year's end, bit by bit they accumulated into small white drifts along steps and roadsides, around trees and posts.

Christal walked a little faster as she headed toward the library. Her hands were shoved into her pockets because she had, as usual, forgotten her mittens. Aunt Ruth would undoubtedly find them on the floor by the front door and be ready to chide Christal when she got home—a well-deserved rebuke, Christal thought as a gust of wind blew tiny snow particles into her face and down the neck of her coat.

Yes, winter was definitely making an entrance.

At least the library would be warm, and she could shed her coat and warm her hands and devote the rest of the day to her reading. Her parents were on a mercy mission to a family in need of assistance, and she had the entire day to herself. She'd even brought an apple to eat so she wouldn't have to go home for lunch.

Today she had things to think about—or to avoid thinking about—and the library was the perfect place. It had become her second home once she'd gotten strong enough to walk the distance by herself, and she went at least once a week. The librarian teased her that one day she would have read every book there, and then what would she do?

Christal's innocent answer had made the librarian laugh: *Weren't there more books being written, more books to buy?*

The library was hushed when Christal entered it. She took a deep breath and filled her nostrils with the glorious smell of books. She headed right to her favorite section, the classic tales of other lands.

She ran her fingers over the golden lettering on the books' spines. Today she was in the mood for something exotic. What would it be? Egypt? The stories of the pharaohs and the sphinx were enticing, but she passed them up. Japan? The history of Commodore Perry's expedition there was exciting, but she had read it three times already. Italy? She loved the tales of ancient Rome, with gladiators and the Coliseum, but not today.

Her hand moved farther along, past the stories, past the poetry, until she came to the history section. She stopped at *Palmetto-Leaves*, a book by Harriet Beecher Stowe. Last year she'd read *Uncle Tom's Cabin*, and the story had moved her greatly. She seized on *Palmetto-Leaves* at once, and opened it and leafed through the pages.

It was about Florida, the St. Johns River, to be exact. She had no idea where the river was or if it was anywhere near Key West, where Isaac was from, but a few pages into the book was a map.

The map cut off the very bottom of Florida, which included Key West, she was sure. But she began to read, and from the first chapter, "Nobody's Dog," she was captured. Stowe was such a good writer that soon Christal was caught up in the book.

At last a rumble from her stomach brought her back from Florida and into Minnesota. Lunchtime.

She placed the book on the table with a whispered message

to the librarian that she would be back to read further, and she stepped out into the glorious November noon. The snow had stopped and the sun shone brightly in a brilliant blue sky. November certainly could be a beautiful month, she thought.

She fished in her bag and withdrew a red apple that she bit into as she walked around the library. It was housed in a splendid building, the Ingersoll Block, and the library took up the entire second floor of the long, narrow structure.

On the main floor were doctors and dentists, those who didn't have home offices like Dr. Bering. She glanced in a window that was undraped to let in the noonday sun and saw a waiting room, its utilitarian furnishings not nearly as grand as those in Dr. Bering's office.

If she were a doctor, would she want to have her office in her home? She mulled it over as she strolled on slowly, enjoying her apple. There would be the issue of transportation, of course. In winter, travel to and from might be difficult, but on days like this, the early days of winter, being out in the sun was wonderful.

Dr. Bering's office had been in his house for so long, he'd probably never thought of moving it out. As it was, the house was still too large for him, even with his office in it. It was good that Isaac was there with him. He would be a great help in cases like John Lawrence's, where the patient became housebound.

She chewed away the last bits of apple from around the core as she thought about her life. It had been perfect, but it was starting to erode around the edges now that she was worried about Mr. Lawrence, whom she'd known for practically her whole life, and there was nothing she could do to help.

Spending her day in the library was not enough, and, in

fact, she felt as if she were idling away her hours there. She should be thinking ahead.

What was her future like? She didn't believe in fortune-telling, but there were times when she'd like a peek into God's plan. What did He have in store for her? Certainly He didn't intend for her to spend the rest of her days in the library reading.

But what was she to do?

She ran through her options.

Could she be a doctor or a nurse and save lives? From what she had learned of the study of medicine from Isaac, she knew she couldn't concentrate to the degree necessary. At her hands, her patients would undoubtedly all fail and die.

She liked ice-skating, but there was no career in that, and besides she wasn't at all good at ice-skating. Her ankles flopped back and forth as if they were made of paper, unless she proceeded very slowly and cautiously.

Music was nice, but her singing voice was dreadful, and she didn't know how to play an instrument. As Dr. Bering had pointed out, she lacked the interest in learning.

Could she be a teacher? Perhaps, but the idea wasn't one she was especially drawn to.

An artist? Her drawings were unrecognizable. A cook? Not when she didn't know how to turn on the stove. A seamstress? She'd have to be able to thread the sewing machine, or at the very least, a needle.

No, she did what she did best, spending her days in the covers of books at the library. A life of idle, self-centered nothingness.

For the past nine years, she'd taken advantage of her illness, although she hadn't done so consciously. Her parents were so glad to have her alive and well, after nearly losing her to death from scarlet fever and rheumatic fever, that they'd taken almost all responsibility away from her.

It had been too easy to coast along, spending days and then weeks and finally years of a life with no responsibility. The time had come for that to end.

She'd nibbled every possible piece of apple from the core, so she wrapped it carefully in her handkerchief and returned it to her bag. She'd throw it away later.

She returned to the library and gave the book back to the librarian. Maybe she'd come back to it another time, but for the moment, the story had lost its allure.

Slowly she put her coat back on and descended the stairs and went out into the November afternoon.

What was she going to do with her life?

She could be married, that much she knew. It was the usual path for women her age, but so far no one had asked for her hand. She didn't quite believe that she was destined to be an old spinster, but the truth was that she was showing about as much promise as a potential wife as an ice-skater or a cook.

For the past year or so, Aunt Ruth had been spending much of the time before church prodding Christal with her bony elbow, pointing out eligible bachelors. Sometimes Christal was sure that there must be something terribly wrong with her aunt's vision. Just two months ago, she had indicated a man who was twice Christal's age.

That wasn't how God meant for it to be done—Christal was sure of that. She wanted to find this man herself, and to fall in love and live happily ever after like her parents, who were still as openly in love now as they had ever been.

So what about Isaac? The question popped into her thoughts and refused to go away.

So what about Isaac? She let her mind drift over the question.

She couldn't get as far as the idea of marrying him, but there was something different about him, something that wasn't like the boys and men she'd met in church.

It was too early to know how it would go with him—if there even was anything to happen. He was a new friend, and she was glad for that.

But if something *could* come of it, well, she would be interested in seeing how it would go.

Maybe there would be more to her life now than reading.

Having an interest in a fellow was new to her, and she had no idea what she was supposed to do.

She grinned. She could ask Aunt Ruth. Somehow she thought the older woman would have hours of advice.

❧

They gathered again in Uncle Alfred's parlor, this time with a plate of gingerbread passing among them. All of them sat in the places they had before, Isaac noted with amusement, just as people sat in the same seats in church week after week.

Christal sat in the rocking chair, her feet tucked under her, and took a piece of gingerbread from the platter. "Thank you so much," she said with a sigh that radiated happiness. "My very favorite food in the world is your spice cookies, Dr. Bering, but your gingerbread comes in a close second." She took a bite and grinned. "They're both especially wonderful this time of year, warming me from the inside out."

"I heard some folks talking at the church today," Rev. Everett said, "that even more snow should come soon."

"Snow?" Isaac sat up straight.

He'd seen snow on the ground now, blown against the corners of the houses and in the cracks of the stone fences on his weekly walk to church, but he hadn't actually seen the snow come down.

The first flakes had fallen while he'd been inside, and he hadn't decided yet if he was glad he'd missed it or if he should have gone out and watched it float down and felt it on his skin. His desire to experience it warred with his concern about the cold. The only time he was truly warm here was when he sat directly in front of the fireplace, and then only one side of him got warm.

His uncle chuckled. "It is November, Isaac. We're heading into winter, and we can expect more snow."

"It gets quite cold here, doesn't it?" Isaac asked. He didn't want to seem like a weakling, worrying all the time about the winter ahead, but the fact was that he didn't truly know what he was in for. He took a measured sip of his tea then asked in a purposefully casual voice, "How cold does it get here, anyway?"

Rev. Everett shrugged. "It's not all that bad. We have houses and fireplaces and blankets, so we make it through all right. I'm sure your uncle will make sure you stay plenty warm here."

Aunt Ruth tapped on the floor with her cane. "The young man asked a question, and he deserves an answer. Alfred, tell him."

His uncle nodded. "You are right as usual, dear Ruth. Sometimes the temperatures do go quite low."

Christal leaned forward. "Like this past January. Remember that?"

"Now, Christal, dear." Mrs. Everett frowned at her daughter. "That wasn't quite the average day. It's not fair to—"

Isaac took a deep breath. What was Christal about to say? He had to know.

He exhaled slowly and asked. "How cold was it?"

Christal looked at everyone and grinned. "It was thirty-six below zero here in St. Paul."

"Thirty-six below zero." He repeated the words slowly. "Thirty. Six. Below. Zero. I can't even imagine what that's like."

"It's cold," Christal said, and everyone laughed. "But it wasn't as cold as it was in St. Cloud the same day. It was fifty below zero there."

"How do you manage when it's like that?" he asked. "Human skin begins to freeze at the same temperature water does, due to the fluid in the cells. If there is wind, we know that increases the danger of frostbite considerably."

He stopped when he realized that the others were staring at him, slight smiles forming on their faces.

"I am sounding like a textbook, aren't I?" he asked. "I am lecturing you all about frostbite, and yet I've never been anywhere that it was even a danger."

"Well, it's a danger here," Aunt Ruth said, "and I daresay you'll see your fair share of blackened fingers and toes."

Isaac bit back the fear that rumbled in his chest.

"Most of the folks here are pretty much aware how dangerous cold weather can be," his uncle said, "but Ruth is right. Every year I do see some frostbite."

"So is it that cold—what was it, fifty below? All winter long?"

"To be exact, the fifty below was in St. Cloud, which is west of us. We were only thirty-six below. But within three days the temperature rose to almost fifty degrees *above* zero." Rev. Everett smiled. "It was very odd."

Isaac's head spun. The numbers swirled around his brain like a bad dream. What had he undertaken?

"There is one advantage to this cold," Dr. Bering said. "The Winter Carnival! If it weren't for our legendary winters, we wouldn't have this opportunity. By the way, I've heard more about it."

Christal stopped chewing, the gingerbread halfway to her mouth. "Tell us!"

"They met on the second, and they've formed a committee."

Aunt Ruth snorted. "That ought to stop it on the spot."

"Oh, not this group," the doctor continued. "George Finch is heading it, and he's a powerhouse of a leader. So far about forty businessmen are on board."

"Who's George Finch?" Isaac asked.

"He's a top-notch leader in our community, and I'm mighty glad he's going to be leading the group. There's also his partner in the wholesale trade, and a banker and a real estate fellow, and many others. It's going to happen." Uncle Alfred folded his hands over his stomach. "And quickly."

"How quickly?" Christal's gingerbread was still poised midair, forgotten.

"Early in the year. I think they're hoping to have it in February. I don't know exactly."

"That's not very long. What are they planning to do in that short amount of time?" Aunt Ruth asked. "Put together a snow fort and have a snowball fight?"

"Snow fort? Not exactly. More like an ice palace."

"Ohhhh." Christal sighed, and a chunk of gingerbread fell onto her skirt, unnoticed. "An ice palace!" She wriggled excitedly. "Just think of it!"

"Christal Maria Everett, please watch yourself. You have gingerbread in your lap," Aunt Ruth said.

"Sorry." She picked it up with her free hand and popped the stray piece into her mouth.

Isaac held up his hand. "Could we stop for just a moment here? An ice palace? What does that mean?"

"In Montreal, they've been having a winter carnival for a while, but they've got smallpox there, so gathering people together isn't going to happen. The fellows who do the ice palace up there, the Hutchinson brothers, are already here, planning for our carnival's palace." His uncle beamed.

"Can they get it done in time?" Mrs. Everett asked.

Uncle Alfred shrugged. "I suppose. We'll have to see. They'll need help here, that's for certain."

They were going to build a palace out of ice. In Minnesota. In the middle of winter. They were insane. Isaac had no doubt about it now.

"Didn't you just tell me that this past New Year's Day it was a balmy thirty-six degrees below zero?" he asked. "I think I'd rather take my chances with smallpox. If the local people want a festival of some kind, why don't they do it in summer, when it's warm?"

"We have the state fair," Christal offered.

"Aren't there any buildings that could house a winter celebration? Surely there must be a large structure of some kind here that would work."

"The idea," his uncle said, "is to have it outdoors."

"Why?"

"Why not?" Uncle Alfred smiled at him.

"No, not 'why not?' Why? Why on earth would you—" Isaac shook his head.

"An ice palace would have to be outside. Otherwise it would melt," Christal said. Her eyes were glowing. "An ice palace!"

"One more time," Isaac said. "An ice palace is outside because it's got to be cold enough to stay frozen. Stay frozen. Did you hear me? Frozen! Who in their right mind would wander around outside to see a palace made of ice?"

"I would." Mrs. Everett spoke up. "I wonder how big it will be. Is the whole thing going to be made of ice?"

"Maybe there'll be a prince," Christal said, her eyes sparkling with laughter. "An ice prince, and—"

"You live in a world of stories," Aunt Ruth said. "There won't be a prince."

Rev. Everett held up his hand. "Not so fast. Christal isn't that far off with her idea. There will be a king and a queen. I heard about it myself at the church. They're Boreas Rex and Aurora, Queen of the Snows."

"Boreas and Aurora," Christal repeated. "What lovely names."

Isaac viewed his companions in the parlor, all apparently sane people who were now preparing to celebrate winter with an outdoor carnival. Could anything be more insane?

"Are these real people?" Isaac asked. "I mean, are there going to be real people crowned?"

"That's what I was told," the minister answered. "And a Fire King, too. He's the enemy of the King and Queen of the Snows."

Christal's face shone with excitement. "This is going to be so much fun!"

How people could enjoy themselves when they were nearly frozen to death was beyond Isaac's imagination. A festival of frostbite, that's what it would be. It would mean more work at his uncle's office. There would probably be a parade of folks with afflicted fingers and toes and noses during the carnival.

"It will be a great boon to the city," Rev. Everett said. "We need something to brighten up those long winter days."

Isaac noticed his uncle regarding him with a definite twinkle in his eyes. "Isaac, you're not quite ready for this, are you?"

He didn't know how to respond. As much as he wanted to argue the point with the Everetts, this wasn't something that was within his control.

Instead of answering, he merely wrung out a faint smile.

It was a crazy idea, this Winter Carnival, but it wasn't his. He needed to let it go and to be supportive as best he could. Debating the merits of an outdoor celebration in the depth of winter wouldn't change anything.

Let it go; let it be, he reminded himself.

The conversation continued until at last Mrs. Everett pointed out that the hour was late, and with a flurry of coats and gloves and scarves, the minister's family was on their way home to the house next door.

His uncle put his arm over Isaac's shoulders as the two of them returned to collect the plates and tidy the parlor.

"Isaac," Uncle Alfred said, "I know it's difficult for you to understand what our life is like up here. But really, it's not that different from Key West. It's colder, of course, but other than that, people are the same wherever you go. They need something to enjoy, something to anticipate."

They could do that indoors, he thought. There was so much wrong with this idea. Not only the cold was a concern, but the fact that the entire carnival was to be put together so precipitously spelled certain failure. Haste did make waste. The proponents of the carnival were ambitious—perhaps too ambitious. The plan was to have this ready in three months?

But one of the lessons he had learned early on in his medical studies was that keeping silent was a talent, one that he had rarely used before embarking on his career. It was, his professor had told the class, the way that learning occurred. One must be silent to listen.

It had been a hard lesson. He had wanted to protest assignments as being overly long and convoluted, but after watching his classmates being chastised for weakness, he had trained himself to keep his opinions private.

He had learned much from his silence, more than he

would have gained from speaking out as he'd often wanted to do. Even certain protocols of treatment, which had seemed laboriously involved and ineffective at first glance, had proven to be important ways of working through a particular illness or malady.

He called upon that now.

Uncle Alfred chuckled. "You're holding your tongue, aren't you? That is something you will need to do quite a bit, you know."

Isaac's stomach twisted uneasily. "I should have done that earlier tonight, shouldn't I?"

His uncle patted him on the back. "Just as you need to understand them, they need to understand you. And you have raised some good questions, and good questions need good answers. Let's hope that there are good answers."

The words reassured Isaac somewhat.

"Get some sleep, my boy," Uncle Alfred said. "Tomorrow comes quickly."

Isaac climbed the stairs to his room, feeling so completely awake that slumber seemed impossible.

He'd taken another of his uncle's books with him, this time a book by a man named Mark Twain. Uncle Alfred had said he'd find the book, *The Celebrated Jumping Frog of Calaveras County and Other Stories*, amusing. Perhaps he could lose himself in the stories. But as he readied himself for bed, the heavy weight of exhaustion fell on him.

He clambered under the covers as quickly as possible to avoid touching the cold wooden floor with his bare feet, his Bible in his hands. The lamp beside him illuminated the pages as he leafed through it in search of some wisdom. He especially liked the Psalms for their praise and comfort. Psalm 4:8 made him smile: *"I will both lay me down in peace, and sleep: for thou, LORD, only makest me dwell in safety."*

Even when it was thirty-six degrees below zero.

With the words of the psalmist in his mind, he closed his eyes, let a prayer settle over his heart, and gave the worries of the day to the Lord.

❧

No music came into Christal's room tonight. The window was closed and latched, as if the early blasts of winter's chill might sneak under the wooden frame with icy fingers and raise the pane.

The evening's conversation swirled in her head, the words as thrilling as the notes of a symphony.

A winter carnival! With a king and a queen and a palace!

She couldn't sit. She walked over to the window and gazed out. The only light on in the house next door was in the parlor, and it soon was extinguished.

How could anyone sleep with this new knowledge?

The palace would be made of ice, her father had said. How would they do it? Would the builders use blocks of ice as if they were bricks? Would it be white when it was done, or would it be transparent?

How big was it going to be? What if it were as big as her house? Even as small as a dollhouse would be wonderful.

She'd never thought about a palace made of ice.

Aunt Ruth was right. It was like a story, one of the fairy tales that she read again and again at the library. But there had never been such a story as this one. And it would be real!

How could she wait?

An ice castle. A snow king and queen. The adversary of fire. It *was* like a story.

An idea flitted into her mind and batted against the edges of her imagination like a butterfly, faintly at first and then with increasing urgency. A story began to take shape.

Maybe she could be a writer! With her love of stories, she could do that.

What would she need to do? She'd have to put these ideas down in words. How hard could it be?

She thought about it more, but it simply wouldn't go past the vague notion of the wonderful images, and she realized that without a plot, the pictures in her mind would stay that way—just pictures.

And she definitely wasn't an artist, so she couldn't transfer them from what she saw in her head to colorful designs on paper.

Christal sighed. She couldn't be a writer, and she couldn't be an artist.

What was she going to do?

The fact was that there weren't a lot of options available to women. Homemaker. Mother. Wife.

She knew that there were some careers open to her. There were writers. She considered Harriet Beecher Stowe, whose book she had been reading at the library. Now there was a woman who was a successful author. *Uncle Tom's Cabin* was a well-known and highly respected book.

There were a smattering of female artists, none of them as popular as their male counterparts, and only a few whose names were familiar to the populace of St. Paul.

It's not that I want to be famous, God, she prayed, *but I'm searching for something to make my life meaningful. I want to make the most of this time here on earth. I could use Your help. If I have a direction, could You guide me to it, please?*

What she really wanted from her life, though, was to make a difference somehow, like Isaac was doing, or was going to do. If only there were a way to somehow have an impact upon another person. Doctors did. Ministers like her father did.

As a woman, her choices were curtailed. Housekeeper, wife, mother. That about summed up her future.

Housekeeper? She looked around her room. Books and papers were piled haphazardly on the floor. Her clothing from the day was draped over the back of the chair. Her hairbrush was on the table, and one shoe was near the window and the other near the door, exactly where they had landed when she'd kicked them off after unbuttoning them.

Wife? Wouldn't she need a husband for that? And if it did happen—she tucked the bright image of Isaac far back into the distant recesses of her mind for the moment—she'd have to know how to do things like cook and sew.

Mother? She thought of her own sweet mother, how she offered advice, how she'd guided Christal through the perilous journey of childhood and into womanhood, how she'd taught her right from wrong. Being a mother was a job that required great things from a woman. Did she have what it would take?

She buried her face in her hands. It was hopeless.

Or was it?

She needed to focus. Even Mrs. Harriet Beecher Stowe, famous novelist though she was, knew how to cook a roast.

It was time she learned.

five

Christal bounced into the kitchen the next morning, filled with resolve. She tied on an apron and said to her mother and aunt, "Teach me to make eggs."

"Only God can make an egg," her father said from behind the newspaper as Aunt Ruth tipped the teapot to fill up her cup.

It was an old joke, but she grinned.

"True, but I am going to make your breakfast egg."

Aunt Ruth stopped midpour. "Excuse me? You?"

"Yes. And I'm going to make the toast, too."

Mother came up behind her and touched her cheek gently. "Dear, I've already prepared breakfast. Your father's egg and his toast are done."

"But I wanted to—"

"Come and sit with us. Your oatmeal is waiting. I made it the way you like it, with brown sugar and cream. Here. Eat it while it's warm before it gets cold."

Her determination crumbled. She did like her oatmeal. Nice and hot, with a sprinkling of sweet brown sugar and a drizzle of cool cream. She started to sit down, but as she did, she remembered her resolution of the night before.

"I need to learn how to do it," she said, standing up again.

Her mother and Aunt Ruth exchanged surprised looks.

"To what do we owe this sudden burst of interest in cooking?" her aunt asked.

Christal stood as straight as she could. "The time has come. I'm old enough that I should know these things."

"Well," her mother said, "that's commendable."

"I'm ready to learn."

"And we are quite pleased," her father said, lowering the paper and folding it carefully, "but the fact is, Christal, breakfast is already made. Perhaps you could embark on breakfast tomorrow."

"You'd have to get up earlier," Aunt Ruth added. "Eggs don't cook themselves."

Mother smiled. "A hard-boiled egg, the way your father likes it, does take twenty-two minutes."

"Twenty-two minutes," Christal echoed faintly.

Her mother smiled. "Oatmeal requires only five minutes to prepare, and putting the toppings on it to make it special doesn't take long at all."

How was it possible that something as delicious as oatmeal took a fraction of the time that a hard-boiled egg did?

"If you're truly interested in learning to cook," her mother said, "you can help me with the noon meal. I'll be roasting a chicken. That's not at all difficult, and it would be a good place to start."

Roast chicken sounded good. She knew how to simply roast it, but her mother added a rub of herbs that made the chicken incredibly delicious.

"We're having the chicken and root vegetables," Mother continued, "and biscuits with gravy. But today we'll start with the chicken and carrots and potatoes. We'll deal with the biscuits another day."

"Not another day," Christal protested. "I want to learn it today."

"Rome wasn't built in a day," her father said as he stood up and carried his dishes from the table.

"I'm not building Rome. I just want to make a meal. All of it."

Papa smiled. "I'll let you womenfolk figure this out. I have a meeting at the church that I'll be late for if I don't hurry along. I'll see you all at noon."

After he left, Mother and Aunt Ruth began clearing the table. Christal scraped the last of her oatmeal from her bowl and stood up to help.

"I'm delighted to see that you've developed a desire to learn about meals," her aunt said as Christal reached for the creamer at the same time the elderly woman did, with the end result that the cream splashed across the linen tablecloth.

Tears stung Christal's eyes. She'd wasted the cream, and the tablecloth would have to be washed. She tried to help, but instead she made more work for her mother and aunt.

"I'm sorry," she said, untying the apron and slipping it over her head. She threw it on the counter in an untidy heap. "I'm so sorry."

Mother quickly came to her side and wrapped her in a soothing embrace. "Christal, my dearest Christal, it's all right."

"No, it isn't." Her voice was muffled against her mother's shoulder. "I've spilled the cream and soiled the tablecloth, and you all must think I am such a clumsy goose."

It was so tempting to let her mother spoil her more, to excuse her deficiencies, but she needed to be strong. She had so much to learn, and at the same time, she had to fight against her own tendency to take the easy way.

"There, there. The creamer was almost empty, and the tablecloth needed to be washed anyway," her mother murmured.

"We all make mistakes," Aunt Ruth said in her no-nonsense voice. "There's no use crying over spilt milk—or spilt cream. It doesn't put it back in the pitcher."

"I won't start preparing the chicken until midmorning," her mother said. "Why don't you go for a walk and get your head cleared, and when you come back, we can discuss what needs to be done to make a nice meal."

"We'll finish up here." Her aunt refolded the napkins at each chair.

Perhaps it was for the better, anyway. If she stayed, she would probably drop a plate or stab herself with a fork.

She fled the dining room and seized her coat from the rack in the front hall. Slipping into it as she left the house, she started up the street, following her usual path toward the library.

"Christal!" Isaac called to her from the doorway of Dr. Bering's house.

She swiped at her nose as surreptitiously as she could. Why was it that the slightest onset of tears made her nose run like a river?

"Yes?"

"Are you going by John Lawrence's house?"

"I wasn't planning on it. Why?" Of course he wanted her to stop and talk when her face was swollen and red from crying. She tucked her chin down and studied the ground beneath her feet as if it were the most fascinating thing in the world.

"Could you do me a favor?" He stepped away from the door a bit and shivered. "I have another bottle of medicine I wanted to get to him, but I don't want him to have to come here, not in this cold. I was going to take it to him, but my uncle had two patients show up this morning, and I'm really needed here."

"Sure, I can take it to him."

"Come on in, then, and I'll give it to you."

He waited until she arrived at the door before going back inside, even though he was in shirtsleeves.

The bottle was on the table by the door.

"He knows how much to take, but if you don't mind," he said, "I'd appreciate it if you could make sure he gets it in him as soon as possible. He told Uncle Alfred two days ago that he was running out, but he didn't come in to get it."

"You're worried, aren't you?" she asked softly.

He tried to look stalwart but failed. "I am," he said at last. "It's not like him."

"I'll take it right over."

"I appreciate it." He walked her to the door. "And Christal, thank you. I don't know how to repay you—"

"Repay me? For what?"

"For doing this. For caring."

"Here's how you can repay me. Pray for Mr. Lawrence."

"I do," he said. "I do."

She believed that he did.

He opened the door and said with delight, "It's snowing!"

"Just barely," she said, unable to keep the merriment from her voice. He sounded like the children in the church seeing the first snow of winter. They'd all run outside and stand like turkeys, stock-still, their heads back, with their mouths open to catch the flakes on their tongues.

"I've never seen it snow before," he said, his voice filled with awe.

"Oh, you have, too!" Christal rubbed her toe in the snow that had drifted up against the stoop. "See? Snow! You silly!"

He smiled at her. "I've never seen it as it was coming out of the sky. I've only seen the icy evidence."

"Well," she said, "you'll see it falling a lot. Wait until it snows big, fluffy, white flakes at sunset. That is absolutely beautiful."

"I can imagine." He wrapped his arms around his torso. "It's beautiful but cold. Brrr! You'd better button that coat!

And don't you have any gloves?"

"Aunt Ruth told you to say that, didn't she?"

He laughed. "She's a smart woman."

"She is."

They stood together, unwilling to part, until at last he shivered wildly. She hadn't even thought about the fact that he was standing outside with her, and he was still in shirtsleeves.

She put her hand on his sleeve. It was slightly damp where the snow had fallen on it. "You're cold," she said, "and I need to get this to Mr. Lawrence."

"Yes," he agreed.

Light snowflakes fell on her eyelashes, and she blinked them away. With a quick nod and smile, she turned and ran down the steps.

As she scurried toward John Lawrence's house, she was aware of Isaac's gaze following her until she was out of his sight.

The day had greatly improved.

The more she knew of Isaac, the more she liked him. He was a caring man, and he was showing that he would probably be a doctor like his uncle, treating the human being as well as the disease.

Her fingers closed tightly over the bottle she was taking to Mr. Lawrence. His cough had punctuated the Sunday service so much that he'd finally had to leave and listen to the sermon from the vestibule. He didn't seem to be getting better.

Her feet sped toward his house, and soon she was at his front door, knocking. "Mr. Lawrence? Mr. Lawrence? It's Christal Everett. I have your medicine from Dr. Bering."

There was no response from inside, and she pounded

on the door. "Mr. Lawrence? Mr. Lawrence? It's Christal Everett!"

A faint sound from within beckoned her to open the door a crack and call again. "Mr. Lawrence? Are you all right? Might I come in?"

A bird's screech from the living room brought her in to see John Lawrence slumped in his chair, his chest rising and falling violently as he gasped for air. From the top of the floor lamp, Aristotle hopped from one leg to the other nervously as she felt for the man's pulse. It was rapid and erratic.

"I'll be right back," she promised him.

She ran out of the house and down the streets until she reached the Bering house. Without knocking, she burst in.

Dr. Bering and Isaac looked up from a sheaf of papers in surprise. "Christal, child, what on earth is the matter?" Dr. Bering asked.

She panted, out of breath and unable to form the words. Instead, she pointed in the direction of the Lawrence residence.

"Your house? Something is wrong at your house?" the doctor guessed.

Isaac was already reaching for his coat. "It's John Lawrence, isn't it?"

Dr. Bering handed his nephew his bag. "Take this. You may need it. I have an appointment with a woman who is due to give birth soon, so I need to stay here. Do you know what to do, Isaac?"

Isaac nodded as he wound a muffler around his neck. "Body temperature, clear airway if necessary, start steam, inhalants as needed." He stared at his gloves. One was brown leather, the other a red and black knit. He shook his head and pulled them on. "I'll figure it out later."

"Have your mother and aunt meet him there," Dr. Bering

said to Christal as Isaac left. "They'll know what to do."

Tears gathered in her eyes. "He's dying, isn't he?"

Dr. Bering patted her shoulder. "He may be. This is why I want your mother and aunt with Isaac."

"He'll know what to do, won't he?" She tried to keep the worry out of her voice but knew she failed.

"I have the greatest confidence in his abilities, but remember that this is new for Isaac. He's just now learning what it's like to work with real people with real problems, not those in the textbooks he had at school. He needs to have those around him who have experience with the ill."

She nodded, numb with the realization of what she had almost done. It was one thing for her to want to find a meaning for her life, to participate as fully as those she loved, but when there was a cost, and such a dear one—she shuddered at the thought.

"I understand," she whispered. "I'll get my mother and Aunt Ruth. I'm sure they'll know what to do."

As she started to leave, he called to her. "Christal, one more thing. Your father is a minister. You've been in the faith since the day you were born. You know what sickness is like, and you also know the strength of the human will. It's a gift from our Lord, this intense love we have for life, the way we cling to it and let go of it so reluctantly. Never underestimate that power."

"I know, and I believe in my heart and in my soul that the body does not last, but we do live on in His presence." She blinked as tears gathered in her eyes. "But it doesn't make it any easier."

He nodded. "I often think, when I see some of the things that befall our bodies, that we are perhaps fortunate to spend eternity without them."

"That's true."

"But let's not send our friend into heaven quite yet." He smiled at her.

She hugged him and hurried next door.

Her mother and Aunt Ruth were just finishing the breakfast dishes. Had all this happened in such a short time? It seemed as if the morning had been going on for quite a long time. She told them what was going on, and the two women quickly whipped off their aprons and walked quickly to the entryway for their wraps.

"Could you finish up for us, Christal?" her mother asked. "There isn't much left to do to bring the kitchen to rights. Just wiping off the last pans and putting away the cutlery."

"I will." Christal chewed on her lip. "He's going to be all right, isn't he? Mr. Lawrence, that is?"

Mother laid her gloves on the table in the hall and took both of Christal's hands in hers. "I hope so, but he is a very ill man, and he's a very old man. Those two factors don't bode well."

Aunt Ruth cleared her throat. "He's much older than I am, but I don't want to be clever about that and pretend that I am still young. I am not. When our bodies age, any sickness takes a greater toll on us than it does when we are young. We don't have quite the resources someone who is, say, in their twenties might have. We're weakening, and it's all part of God's plan."

Christal turned to her aunt, who stood tall and straight, as stately as ever. For the first time, she noticed the beginning of wrinkles on her face and neck, the white strands that sprinkled the upswept dark hair. Had she been so absorbed in herself that she hadn't noticed the changes in those around her?

Aunt Ruth settled her scarf and met Christal's gaze with her eyes still as sharp and shining as bright black buttons. "Don't worry, Christal. I am in excellent health. When the good Lord decides to take me, I suspect He will do so as quickly as possible, probably to avoid the potential that I might argue with Him otherwise. I do enjoy living, and I have no intention of leaving this earth anytime soon."

"We must hurry," Mother said. "Christal, I don't know how long we will be gone, so could you please stay? If we're not back when your father comes home for his noon meal, there is enough beef left that if sliced carefully, can serve both of you. A cold meal won't hurt either of you. There's bread in the box, of course. And butter in the—"

Aunt Ruth tapped her cane on the floor. "Sarah, if you insist upon giving the girl an inventory of what's in the kitchen, we may never get there. She is smart enough to figure it out herself."

"That's true." Mother kissed Christal's forehead. "I'm sorry about the cooking lesson being delayed, but I think you understand."

Christal nodded. There were a few things more important than a roast chicken.

The two women left, and suddenly the house, which Christal had lived in for most of her life, seemed large and empty. There was nothing to do except get busy.

She returned to the kitchen and picked up the apron she'd discarded earlier. Of course she had dropped it on the counter, but her mother had picked it up and hung it on the hook by the door.

She pulled it over her head and tied it in the back and looked at the task she'd been left.

There were two pans left to dry and a handful of forks and spoons to be put into the drawer. It would take her moments to finish that.

Maybe she should address the beef and the carrots that her mother had told her about. There was no use waiting until the very last minute.

She dug them out of the icebox and examined them. The piece of beef that her mother referred to didn't seem as if it would feed one person, let alone two. The carrots were fine, but her father couldn't have a meal of carrots only.

She took the towel from the rack and dried the remaining two pans, put them away, and sorted the forks and spoons into the appropriate slots in the cutlery drawer.

Again, she regarded the little bit of food that was available to her. Unless she was to serve her father a carrot sandwich, she'd have to think of something else.

She peeked in the icebox again. Ah. There it was. The solution.

&

"Inhale."

Isaac placed his hand on John Lawrence's chest. There was almost no muscle tone, and he could easily feel each rib as the man tried to breathe.

His uncle should have come. He wasn't prepared to see a patient on his own, especially one this ill. This was a doctor's realm, and he was a mere student.

From the kitchen came the subdued sounds of Mrs. Everett and Aunt Ruth as they tidied up the kitchen and boiled water to make steaming vats to place around the patient.

"Don't fight it. Go ahead," Isaac urged. "Breathe in, as deeply as you can."

"I'll cough," Mr. Lawrence said in a weak voice.

"Then cough. You need to. It's the way your body clears out the infection that's clogging your lungs. Take a deep breath, as full as you can. Go past the urge to cough."

"Can't." The older man bent over as a series of spasms jerked his torso.

He was clearly fighting the cough, and Isaac didn't blame him. Mr. Lawrence's throat was raw from it, and his entire being was simply tired of it.

Isaac knelt. "I want to make sure you're getting enough oxygen. The problem with what you have is that inhaling triggers the cough reflex, so you're breathing very shallowly. Let's try it two different ways. First, breathe in slowly."

Mr. Lawrence took a breath and stopped as a cough burst out.

"That's fine. Let's try this then," Isaac said. "Breathe in as rapidly and deeply as you can."

Mr. Lawrence tried it, and only at the end did he cough.

"Good! I'm not saying you can breathe like that all the time—it'd be a neat trick if you could, but you'd end up so light-headed you might faint—but I'd say every couple of minutes, if you could do that, your body would appreciate it."

For a few minutes, the two men breathed together, the strong lungs and the weak lungs, in unison as if one could lend the other some of his vigor.

"I do feel a bit better," the patient said at last.

Isaac laughed. "I'm not surprised. Our bodies need oxygen. It feeds our brains and our blood and our muscles. I wish I had some way to pipe it into you, but I don't."

As he settled the man into an upright position, pointing out that he'd be more likely to breathe better if he were sitting up straight, he talked to him about his illness.

"You have heavily congested lungs. I'd like to dry them out, but that very act of drying them out will cause increased coughing, and you're quite cachectic."

"Of course I am," Mr. Lawrence said with a little smile. "What on earth does that mean?"

"I'm sorry," Isaac answered, mentally reviewing one of the lessons of medical school, that a doctor should speak using words that the patient will understand and avoid terminology that is specific to physicians. "I mean simply that your body as a whole is suffering."

It wasn't a true definition. What it meant was that the patient was wasting away. His skin was thin, only a loose covering over his skeleton. He was so gaunt that every bone showed. There was no muscular definition.

It was the circular dilemma of a major illness. Because he was sick, his body was atrophying. And because it was atrophying, he couldn't fight the illness. He didn't have the strength.

"Your uncle and I have talked quite a bit about death. He has told me I'm dying." Mr. Lawrence's voice was reedy, like a child's.

"He did?" Isaac stopped midmotion. In his studies, he had been taught that one should never tell a patient that he was dying. One reason was that it might not be true, and the other was that patients often simply gave up upon hearing the news.

Mr. Lawrence's chuckle sounded like wind through dry grasses, and he stopped for a paroxysm of coughing. "I'm sorry," he said at last. "I'll have to do that inhalation business you showed me."

Isaac nodded. "Indeed."

"You seemed surprised that your uncle was blunt with me. Am I right?"

Isaac pondered how to respond. He didn't want to make Uncle Alfred look bad in the eyes of his patient, but he was curious as to why he'd said such a thing. "You and my uncle go back quite a ways, I understand," he said at last, opting for a nonanswer.

"We do. I've got some illness in my lungs, and it's got one of those names that I couldn't pronounce for the life of me, no pun intended. But here's what else I know, and what your uncle knows. I'm eightysomething—I quit counting birthdays long ago—and I'm looking at heaven. As a matter of fact, I'm right at the gate. I can even peek through the slats and see the other side."

Isaac smiled at the old man's imagery.

"Everybody my age is nearing the end anyway, but when you're my age and sick. . ." Mr. Lawrence shrugged, and a round of coughing took over. "Your uncle is younger than I am, but he and I did indeed discuss being at our stage of life, when our bodies fail. We're like old wagons. Oh, maybe our wheels don't fall off, but the axle sure gets cracked. At some point, we're past the point of repair."

"Oh, I don't believe that," Isaac said heartily. "Medicine is doing quite a bit of wonderful things and soon—"

"Soon we'll live to be as old as Methuselah? What does the Bible say? How old was he?"

"Nine hundred sixty-nine years." Isaac grinned. "Everybody back then lived for a long time. Jared was 962 years old when he passed on. Lamech was 777 years old when he died."

Mr. Lawrence waved it away. "Older than I'd want to be. Can you imagine what a thousand-year-old man would look like? What could he do? Do I want a couple hundred years of mashed food?"

Aristotle, who'd been sleeping through most of the ministrations, woke up and flew across the room, raucously shrieking as he barely missed Isaac's head.

"And besides, unless my dear Aristotle can live long, too, why would I want to?"

Mr. Lawrence was smiling when he said it, but Isaac knew

how attached he was to his bird. And the heart, when it lacked a reason to go on beating, often simply stopped.

"I reminded your uncle that although I may not last here on earth much longer, I have a home awaiting me in heaven," Mr. Lawrence continued. He wheezed and coughed, and Isaac knew the discussion was wearing him out. But it was all right. He needed to say what he was saying.

"That's very true."

"Is the minister's wife in the kitchen? Is that her I hear rattling around in there?"

"She and Ruth Everett are both in there."

"Will you ask Sarah to come out here?"

Isaac stood and went into the kitchen.

"How's he doing?" Mrs. Everett asked.

"He's very sick, but I think we can make him comfortable. He needs to have some nutrition for one thing, so if you could make some broth to start, that would be great. Of course, the steam pots will help clear the congestion, too."

"I can do that. I'll run home and get that chicken and start stewing it," Ruth said. "It'll make good stock and some healthy soup when he's up for it."

"That sounds good. Meanwhile," he said to Christal's mother, "he's asking for you."

"For me?"

She took off her apron and hurried into the parlor. "John, what can I do for you?"

"You're a Bible-toting woman."

"I believe you could call me that." She looked at Isaac, her eyes brimming with amusement. "Just as you're a Bible-toting fellow."

"I am, but I'm too spent at the moment to locate what I want to hear now. Can you find me that part about what heaven is like? You know, the verses about our future homes being mansions?"

" 'In my Father's house are many mansions'?"

"That's the one. You don't need the Bible for this one, do you?"

"I don't. It's a beautiful passage. It's from John 14. 'Let not your heart be troubled: ye believe in God, believe also in me. In my Father's house are many mansions: if it were not so, I would have told you. I go to prepare a place for you. And if I go and prepare a place for you, I will come again, and receive you unto myself; that where I am, there ye may be also.'"

"I'm going there—you know that, don't you?" he asked.

Isaac stood off to the side, wanting to be respectful.

Mrs. Everett touched Mr. Lawrence's arm. "Oh, John, I hope we all are. We just arrive at different times."

"I'll be there before you."

She fussed with the cloth of his sleeve. "Maybe. God will take us when it's our time to go. Until then, though, we need to live as fully as we can here on earth."

Mr. Lawrence coughed, and Isaac reached out to give him his medicine. Mr. Lawrence held up his hand in objection.

"The medication will give you relief from the coughing," Isaac said.

"It makes me sleepy. I take it, and almost immediately I fall asleep."

"Yes, it will do that," Isaac answered. "It's formulated for that very purpose. It has an ingredient that lets you sleep."

"Lets me sleep? Makes me sleep!" Mr. Lawrence's words were grumbling, but a small smile twitched at the edges of his mouth.

"You need to rest." Isaac offered the spoon again, and the patient shook his head.

"I'll make sure he takes it," Christal's mother said.

"I'm going to get lectured, aren't I?" Mr. Lawrence asked mournfully.

"You are. You need to do exactly as the doctor orders. Take your medicine now. Later Ruth will bring you some broth, and I will sit here myself and make sure you drink it. After the broth, we'll graduate you to soup."

"And from there, on to pork chops!" Coughing caught at the laughter and stopped it.

"Yes, pork chops."

There was nothing more for Isaac to do at the moment. With the medicinal syrup at work in Mr. Lawrence's exhausted system, he'd soon sleep. Already the man's eyes were hooded with fatigue, and his breathing, with the coughing spasms eased, was regular and, Isaac was gratified to see, deeper, getting oxygen to his starved cells.

"You can go," Mrs. Everett said at last. "I'll stay with him."

"Thank you."

He knew that John Lawrence would be in good hands with her at his side. The woman had the soul of a saint. She could handle any emergency that came her way.

Christal's aunt came to the door between the living room and the dining room. "Isaac, I hate to take you away from the business of doctoring, but I'd like to get the chicken soup started so it's ready when John wakes up. Everything is here except the chicken." She chuckled. "It's pretty important to have chicken in your chicken soup. If you wouldn't mind, could you go to our house and pick up the chicken? Oh, and a few more potatoes and carrots. John's produce bin is looking a bit spare. Christal's home. She'll put it all in the stockpot for you."

Isaac's heart lightened. He knew what awaited him

at the Everett house. Christal's buoyant good spirit, her indefatigable joy of living, and her bright happiness with life in general lifted his mood every time. After a struggle like today, he needed her effervescence.

He hurried his way there, smiling as he imagined her shining face.

At the house, he knocked on the door and waited, tapping his fingers against each other in anticipation.

There was no answer.

He knocked again. Still, no one came to the door.

His disposition lost its glow. She must have left the house.

Still, the chicken was needed. Perhaps she hadn't locked the door when she left? He turned the handle of the heavy door cautiously, and it swung open.

Immediately he reeled at the smell. It hung in the air, acrid and sharp. Something had been on fire.

"Christal? Christal?"

He clapped his hand over his nose and mouth and tried to breathe shallowly, which was nearly impossible in his abrupt state of panic.

"Christal?" he called again, and then, with more urgency, again. "Christal!"

His heart leaped into his throat and beat rapidly. Christal hadn't come to the door. Could it have been because she was unable to?

The thought stabbed him, and he nearly doubled over from the pain. But a rush of sudden energy gave wings to his feet, and he sprinted through the house, following the bitter cloud that hovered over his head. Within seconds he was at the source of the smell.

A haze hung in the kitchen, and the odor was dreadful. Christal stood at the counter, her hair sliding out of the braid at the back of her neck. Her apron was festooned with multicolored stains, and a smudge of black ran across her nose. A curl of carrot peel was stuck over her ear, and shreds of potato skins lay scattered around her feet.

At her side in an instant, he enveloped her in his arms, carrot peelings and all, and buried his face against the top of her head. "Christal, you're not injured, are you? Was there a fire? Were you burned? If you are, I could, you know, I'm a doctor, or almost, and—oh, my dear, my dear, my dear."

He knew he was babbling, but he couldn't stop. If anything had happened to her—it was too much to even consider.

"I'm fine." She sniffled against his chest.

Relief mingled with love, he murmured wordlessly as he held her against him. His mouth moved over her head in a series of kisses that flowed like water.

Dear God, thank You! She isn't injured, she isn't burned, and she's in my arms. Dearest God, thank You!

The smell was distinct around her, and even more so as he buried his lips into her hair.

"What's burned?" he asked, pulling back a bit. "It smells like—it smells like hair! Like burned hair!"

"It might be." Christal sniffed and wiped the back of her hand across her cheek, leaving yet another dark smear.

"Is it—*your* hair?" Isaac asked cautiously. The kitchen was a terrible mess. Bits and pieces of food were everywhere, and water pooled on the floor in front of the stove. And above it all, the sharp reek of burned hair permeated the air.

"Yes."

She turned and showed him the awful truth. A section of her hair, over her left eye, was singed off. A short bit, perhaps an inch and a half, stuck straight out, the ends ragged and uneven where they'd been burned.

"I made a little mistake. I'm not sure exactly how."

"Here, sit down." He guided her to the little table at the end of the counter and pulled out a chair for her and one for himself. "Can I get you a drink of water?"

She nodded and waved toward the counter. "I was going to make some tea."

"Did you burn your hair then?" he asked, getting up to find an empty cup and a tin of tea next to it. The water was hot on the back of the stove—probably, he thought, a way of keeping the room warm at the same time—and he opened drawers until he found a tea ball. He made a pot of tea and then poured them both cups.

She wrapped her hands around the cup as if seeking the warmth.

"What happened?" he asked again.

She looked at him, her blue eyes filled with tears. "I was burning the feathers off the chicken."

He had no idea what she was talking about. "Christal," he began, realizing he was in uncharted waters, "this chicken had feathers?"

"All chickens do," she said. She stared at him, as if he had taken total leave of his senses.

He tried to redeem himself. "Well, I know they start with feathers. I understand, however, that one plucks a chicken rather than burning the feathers off."

She nodded.

"And," he continued, "I don't know anything about cooking a chicken, but I'm pretty sure they come with their feathers already off. This one didn't?"

"Most of them. But my mother always burns off the pinfeathers," she said. "I've seen her. She singes them off."

"How?" He almost dreaded the answer.

"She uses a match."

"And you caught your hair on fire doing that?"

She shook her head. "No."

"Then how did you do it?"

She sighed. "I had peeled the potatoes and scraped the carrots. I was going to put them in the stockpot, but then I remembered that I'd done it backwards, that Mother always started the chicken first. So I pushed them aside, and I got the match, and I singed off the pinfeathers just fine."

He rested his chin on his hand. He adored this woman, but she was taking forever to get to the point. "And the fire?" he prompted.

She shrugged. "I got too close to the match, and the next thing I knew, I was on fire." She looked sadly at the disarray around her. "I made a mess—a mess of the kitchen and a mess of myself. And everything smells really bad, doesn't it?"

"I am not going to lie to you," he said, smiling at her. She really looked pitiful, sitting at the table, trying to stick her singed hair back into place and being quite unsuccessful. "Yes. Burned hair is quite, um, aromatic, shall we say?"

As much as he would have liked to linger and talk with her, he had a mission to fulfill—getting the chicken for Christal's aunt to make soup with. He spoke to her of it.

"Take it," Christal said, pushing the stockpot toward him. "You're lucky you got here when you did, or it would have been ruined."

He glanced inside and saw a sad-looking chicken, its skin charred here and there, evidence of her failed culinary efforts.

She sat up suddenly as the grandfather clock in the parlor chimed. "Oh, no! Papa will be home in minutes, and look at this place! Look at me! Nothing is ready for him to eat!"

She leaped to her feet and began sweeping up the mess on

the kitchen floor. "Put the vegetables in the pot and run the chicken to Aunt Ruth, please, and let me get this place put to rights!"

He took the heap of scraped carrots and potatoes, added them to the pot, and put the lid on the top. His muffler had gone awry, and he began to straighten it, turning to say good-bye to her.

She was on her knees on the floor again, trying to scoop up the fallen potato peelings, and from the audible sniffling, he knew she was crying again.

"Let me help." He dropped to the floor beside her and gathered up the scrapings for her.

"I wanted to help," she said, wiping the back of her hand across her eyes. "That's all I wanted to do today was help. Nobody wanted my help. Not you, not your uncle, not my mother, not my aunt, nobody. So I tried to do something on my own, something that would be helpful, and look what I did! And now you want to help me? I can't do anything on my own."

He took her hands in his, ignoring the stray peelings and scrapings that adorned their wrists and fingers. "Christal, it's a matter of learning," he said, "and that in itself has its own run of fits and starts. You'll learn to cook by your mistakes as well as your successes. I'm sure that's how your mother learned. We all do."

"My mother's perfect."

He chuckled. "She may be, but I suspect that she had her trials along the way, too. She has, I'm sure, burned toast and oversalted stew."

"Maybe," she said, her voice brimming with doubt, "but when I compare myself to her. . ."

He stood up. "I have to get this chicken to the Lawrence

household, but before I go, I want to remind you that comparing yourself to your mother is probably not the best idea. She has much more experience than you do. I suspect that what makes us all better at everything we do is actually doing it, getting the experience."

"And praying that you don't catch anything on fire," she added morosely.

"That, too."

Together they added the last of the ingredients to the pot, a pungent onion and three smashed garlic cloves.

Within minutes, he was on his way to John Lawrence's house, the filled stockpot in his hands.

Mr. Lawrence still slept soundly, he was gratified to see. Mrs. Everett sat beside him, humming softly. Isaac handed the pot to Aunt Ruth, who made a face. "That's a strong onion!"

He breathed a sigh of relief. The onion had covered whatever smell of smoke might be lingering on him.

After reassuring himself that Mr. Lawrence was stable, he hurried back to his uncle's house.

He'd have to focus on the patients at hand and get his mind off the feeling of Christal in his arms.

He'd known her such a short time. He needed to rein in his feelings for her. She was a minister's daughter, after all, and although he'd never romanced one before, he was sure that the daughter of a churchly man would require a slower approach. Plus there was the fact that any courting would have to wait until he finished his studies.

Nevertheless, what had he done? He'd kissed her! Not on the lips, but that nuzzling the top of her head was kissing as sure as the sun rose each day.

He shouldn't have, but it seemed so right.

"How's John?" Uncle Alfred asked when Isaac entered the house, rubbing his hands together to warm them.

"He's congested, and his lungs are filling." The answer was short but to the point. The image of Christal was driven from his mind and replaced with the thin face of John Lawrence. "He's failing."

Isaac dropped onto the overstuffed chair and buried his face in his hands. "How do you do this, Uncle? How?"

Uncle Alfred walked to him and patted his shoulder. "In order to be strong in death, we have to believe in life. You believe in life, don't you?"

"Yes." His answer was muffled against his locked fingers as he willed himself not to cry.

The only sound was the ticking of the clock atop the cabinet. Isaac breathed deeply and sat up. It wouldn't do for him to lose control like this.

"Sometimes the patient will die. Despite our best efforts, despite our best medicines, the patient will die." His uncle sighed and stared hard into the fireplace. The dancing flames were reflected in his tired eyes. "Every time that happens, my faith is tested, Isaac. I wonder how a God who loves His people, a God who gave them life, can take it away from them, and often with great suffering."

Neither of them spoke. A log fell and sparked, sending tiny glimmers of light onto the hearth, where they burned out quickly.

It's a metaphor, Isaac mused. We're like those little pieces of the log, beautiful and shining as we arc through the air, and yet we end as ashes on the brick, burned, with only the ash to show that we were ever there.

"Except for memories," Dr. Bering said, and Isaac realized that he'd spoken his thoughts aloud. "People stay on in the lives of others. They've shaped the people around them by loving them, or, in some cases, by hating them—or perhaps worst of all, by their indifference."

Isaac frowned. Indifference?

"Ignoring the cries of your fellow human beings is reprehensible," his uncle continued. "It is a sin beyond sin. But fortunately, most of our lives are formed by the love around us. Parents who love us, siblings, relatives, friends, spouses—every time we are told we're loved, either in word or action, we are strengthened and bettered."

"Christal's mother and aunt are there with Mr. Lawrence, tidying and making chicken soup."

His uncle chuckled. "He's in good hands then. So what did you do to treat John?"

Isaac ran through the regimen he'd prescribed, and his uncle nodded approvingly. "Good. That's perfect."

Uncle Alfred motioned toward the examination room. "Now we go from near-death to near-life. I'd like you to meet Mrs. Bonds. I think we can expect a Christmas baby from her."

❧

Christal bent down and swooped up the last stray carrot peeling before leaning against the stove and wiping her forehead. At last, the kitchen didn't show the signs of the chaos that had occurred. The smell of her burned hair still hung in the air a bit, but it was dissipating. She'd opened every window in the house, and a beeswax candle lit in the kitchen was helping to disperse the odor.

She tucked the burned part back into the other hair at her temple and pulled a pin out from the bun at the nape of her neck and used it to keep the short section in place. Stuck in at the right angle, the pin might hide the singed area well.

The memory of being held by Isaac flooded back, as real and palpable as if he were still there. She could feel the imprint of his fingers in her hair as he soothed her. Had he—had he kissed her head? Or had she wanted it so badly that she imagined it?

If he *had* kissed her—the thought made her smile.

She had liked it very much, being close to him. Maybe it might happen another time, and it might even be on the lips.

She hugged herself, as if doing so could keep the event fresh in her mind.

He'd kissed her! Or, she corrected herself, he maybe kissed her!

"Are you cold?" Her father spoke from the doorway of the kitchen, startling her so much that she nearly jumped.

She shook her head. "Sorry! I didn't hear you come in. I've got your meal all laid out. It's not much."

As they walked together into the dining room, she filled him in on the events of the day.

Her father frowned, but as he said the blessing over the food, he included the line, "And we pray for those who are sick and for those who tend to the sick."

They ate quickly, because, as he explained to her, the Christmas charity group was meeting and he had to return to the church.

"I'm hoping to get Isaac on the team," he said as he stood up after eating. "He'd be—oh! I nearly forgot. Come with me."

She followed her father to the entryway, where he reached into the pocket of his overcoat and handed her a small tin. "I don't know what this is about," he said. "Isaac stepped out of the door of his uncle's house and asked me to give you something. Then he went back inside and got this."

He put his coat on and wrapped a scarf around his neck.

"I know, I know," he said with a grin. "I'd better button up, because if I don't, as sure as anything I'll see Aunt Ruth!"

With those words and a hasty peck on his daughter's forehead, Papa was gone.

She looked at the tin curiously. Ornate flowery golden letters spelled out GARDEN DELIGHT HAIR POMADE. She opened it, and a faintly familiar scent floated up.

Why did she know this aroma? Where had she smelled it?

six

The next two weeks were filled with a flurry of activity. Christal's usual trips to the library were curtailed as she worked on becoming knowledgeable about homemaking. She stood in the kitchen every morning and evening, trying to learn the fine art of cookery. Her motivation was real and her mother was patient, but there seemed to be so much to remember.

Baking soda and baking powder were actually two different products, and cream of tartar had nothing to do with cream. Egg whites were actually clear until they were cooked, and separating an egg required steady hands.

A pinch was bigger than a smidgen, and a sprinkle could mean one shake or two, depending on whether she was adding cinnamon, which required two shakes, or salt, which took only one.

Two cups made a pint—or was that a quart? Were there sixteen tablespoons to a cup measure? And which was the bigger one, the teaspoon or the tablespoon? The numbers spun in her head until she'd gotten the idea to write everything down in a little book she kept in her apron pocket—her own personal guide to the art of cookery.

At last the evening came when she leaned over the stove and pulled out a pork roast that was fragrant with herbs and oil. It was beautiful and smelled wonderful. The proof, of course, was with the tasting, and she held her breath as, at the dinner table, her father stood to slice into it with great ceremony.

He served each of them a piece, and as one, they all tried it.

The meat was done perfectly, tender and aromatic, and she smiled with relief as her family congratulated her. She felt ridiculously happy. She'd done it!

She'd never mentioned the incident with the chicken, although she suspected that her mother and aunt knew something was amiss from the burn marks on the bird, but neither had said a word. She'd managed to get the kitchen back to its usual pristine state by the time her father had gotten home, and had, in fact, made a quite passable lunch of cold beef with carrots and bread and butter for him.

They had just finished their meal of the pork she'd roasted and she was putting the dishes away when a knock sounded at the door.

"I'll get it," her father said.

The voices of their next-door neighbors carried into the kitchen.

"Isaac is here!" Christal said, untying her apron and flinging it onto the small table. She stopped and grinned sheepishly at her mother and aunt. "I know, I know. I'll hang it up."

She retrieved the apron and put it on the hook properly. She left the kitchen, then slowed, smoothing down the front of her dress and checking the hall mirror to make sure the burned lock of hair wasn't sticking straight out. From her position in the hallway, she could hear her mother and Aunt Ruth.

"She's learning quickly," Mother said, and Christal smiled at the pride in her mother's voice. She pulled herself up straighter and walked toward the parlor. "Something in her has changed, and I'm very pleased with what she's doing. Whatever her motivation is, it's working."

"She's in love," Aunt Ruth said, and Christal stopped so suddenly she almost tripped.

"Do you think so? They've just met, although—" Her mother's voice continued but became too faint for Christal to hear. She must have moved to the far side of the kitchen.

Aunt Ruth's voice was strong enough to carry, though. "I knew immediately when I met my Theo at the skating party that he was the one for me. And the minute Matthew laid eyes on you, dear Sarah, he was smitten and has remained so."

Her mother said something that Christal couldn't quite make out, and her aunt responded with vigor, "Love at first sight, or love at hundredth sight. It doesn't matter. Love is love."

Was it possible? She had barely seen Isaac since the fiasco with the chicken, and when they had been together, they had either been at church or in passing outside. She had finally convinced herself that the kisses on the top of her head had merely been flights of fancy and that she had imagined them.

The question was: *Why had she imagined them?* Could it have been because she wanted them so badly that she had let her mind create them?

Was it because she was in love with Isaac Bering?

Her heart fluttered a bit at the thought.

From the parlor she heard his laughter. Her pulse raced, and the palms of her hands grew sweaty.

Maybe her aunt was right, but that wasn't why she was learning the fine art of housekeeping—was it?

"Are you waiting for an invitation from the queen herself?" Her father stood at the door of the parlor. "Come on! Dr. Bering has brought more of the spice cookies you enjoy so much."

"I'll be in soon," she answered, marveling at how calm and collected she sounded. "If he has cookies, we'll need tea. I'll help get it ready."

"Don't take long!" he said before he vanished back into the parlor.

She turned to go back into the kitchen and met her mother and aunt on the way out. Her mother held a tray with a teapot and cups on it.

"How did you manage that?" she asked. "I just now said that—"

"Christal, dear, what your mother heard was the sound of guests coming. One always prepares tea for guests," Aunt Ruth chided a bit harshly, and Christal felt herself coloring from the rebuke.

"It wasn't difficult to do," Mother said with her usual gentleness. "The water was already hot. Tea is the easiest beverage in the world to make, I believe."

"Christal, there is much you need to know." Her aunt's tone was brisk but loving. "This is simply a fact, something every woman should be aware of. It's a matter of etiquette."

"Men don't have to make tea," Christal muttered. "Don't they have to be polite?"

Her mother ducked her head, but not before Christal saw the smile on her face.

"Well, of course they do." Aunt Ruth put her arm around her niece's shoulders. "Don't you hear your father in there? He's making our guests feel welcome by talking to them. It's just Alfred and Isaac, but your father's had to develop the talent of carrying on a conversation with anyone and making them feel like they're his favorite people. Sometimes, Christal, what seems the easiest can be the hardest."

Christal's spirits flagged. Just as she took one step forward, she realized that there was a whole flight of steps ahead of her, like a stairway of life. How would she ever catch up? How many times had she seen her parents in exactly this situation, her father talking with the guests in the parlor as her mother made tea and served it? Yet she'd never taken notice of it.

She would never catch up. She should have started a long time ago, paying attention to the operations of the house.

Well, she'd gotten as far as learning to make a savory pork roast, and she already knew how to brew a pot of tea, and she was remembering to hang her apron on its hook when she was done, but that wouldn't be good enough when she had her own household to tend to, unless she and her husband wanted to live on pork and tea.

Her own household! Her husband!

Like wild butterflies, her thoughts flew back to Isaac. It was easy—too easy, perhaps—to imagine him in the role, sitting in his chair in the parlor reading the newspaper. Or across the table from her, eating his roast pork and drinking his tea. Or greeting her each morning with a kiss.

"If we're going to serve this tea, we really should be in the same room as our guests," her mother prompted, her eyes twinkling.

Her mother led them into the parlor. The men all stood when the women came in. Isaac looked directly at Christal, and suddenly she felt as awkward as a schoolgirl.

Is that what love is like, God? she asked silently. *Is it being flustered and tongue-tied around him?* She glanced over and noticed how her mother's eyes immediately focused on her father, and the slow smile that curved her lips spoke volumes—silently.

She couldn't stop herself from sliding her gaze over to Isaac, who now sat on the small sofa. Heat climbed up her neck and onto her cheeks in a sudden flush, and beads of sweat sprang out on her upper lip, and of course, the singed section of her hair chose that moment to escape the pins that held it back. She could see it on the periphery of her sight, its edges poking straight out as if it were waxed.

Isaac stood up so quickly that his shins knocked into the table in front of him, and Mother had to steady the cups she was in the process of placing there.

"I'm sorry," he said to her, and as he tried to assist, he succeeded only in clinking them together and dislodging them from their saucers.

"It's fine," Mother said. "No harm done."

He stepped away and sat back down self-consciously as she put the tray back to rights and then took her place beside her husband. "I'll—" he began, but Aunt Ruth interrupted him.

"Excuse me," she said, stepping around Christal and taking a seat in the chair covered in ruby-toned velvet.

Christal stared at her aunt. Plush and soft, with deeply carved wooden arms—the chair was always hers. Her aunt liked to sit on the small sofa near the fireplace. Where Isaac was now sitting. Where the only empty seat was. Where she was going to have to sit.

Apparently he realized it at the same time she did, for he stood up again and nodded as she crossed the room to join him.

They both sank to the sofa together, and Christal kept her body as rigid as possible, trying to avoid squishing herself against him. The sofa was small, though, and coziness was unavoidable.

She tried not to think about the fact that he was so close to her, so close that she had no choice but to let her elbow touch his. It was either that or she'd have to crane herself backward or hunker over forward. Well, she told herself, if it didn't bother him, it didn't bother her.

She was not a good liar.

This close to him, she could smell the clean fragrance of soap and bay rum. It certainly was an improvement over their encounter in the kitchen, when the air had been full of the awful smell of burned hair. Her fingers stole up to her temple, and she tucked the singed lock back under the safety of the hairpin that tried to conceal the damage.

The conversation drifted from one topic to another, until at last Dr. Bering asked if a family had been selected for the church's goodwill project.

Her father shook his head. "We had a family selected, but they left to go back to Indiana, so we're without one at the moment. We'll need to find someone else, and quickly."

Dr. Bering leaned back and laced his fingers across his stomach. "Could I make a suggestion? I have in mind a young couple expecting their first child. They're as poor as church mice but quite pleasant and kind. I don't believe they have a church home yet, so this would be a good way to reach out to them."

Papa nodded thoughtfully. "That sounds splendid. I'll stop in tomorrow morning, if you don't mind, and pick up the details."

"It would be perfect for the season, wouldn't it, Matthew?" Mother said softly. "So reminiscent of the first Christmas."

"Except this woman won't be giving birth in a stable, I can assure you of that," the doctor said with a deep chuckle. "Not in these days and times!"

"That new hospital is supposed to be quite the place, I understand," Papa said, and Aunt Ruth agreed.

"It's got the latest gizmos and gadgets, everything a doctor could want or need," she said, grinning at Dr. Bering. "All a physician has to do is push a button, and the machine takes it from there."

"Not exactly," Dr. Bering responded with a chortle. "And even if it were so, Ruth, someone still has to know which button to push!"

Christal's mind began to wander away from the subject of hospitals and charity cases. How could she concentrate on something like that when Isaac was so near that she could feel him breathing, the rise and fall of each inhalation and exhalation?

Usually the only time she was this close to a man who was not related to her was at church—and then only at the Christmas and Easter services, when the sanctuary was packed with visitors and with those who made the trek to worship on the holidays. Then the pews were filled to capacity with a suddenly large congregation.

That wasn't the same. This, no, this was different.

The sound of the others' voices was a background to her thoughts, and to the rhythm of Isaac's breathing.

She couldn't focus on anything except him.

Oh, this wasn't good. Not good at all.

Was this what God meant for her? Was she supposed to fall in love with Isaac Bering?

He seemed to be fond of her, if indeed her recollection of the time in the kitchen after the great hair catastrophe had occurred, and he had truly nuzzled her hair as he held her. The more she thought about it, the more likely it seemed that her memory was correct.

He laughed, and she nearly jumped out of her skin. What had someone said that was funny? She had totally lost the conversation.

"Wouldn't you agree?" her father asked her.

She had no idea what to say. What on earth were they talking about? Everyone was watching her, including Isaac, who had turned his head and was looking at her curiously.

"Well," she said slowly, hoping that if she were vague enough, no one would know she'd been woolgathering, "you know me."

"I believe we do," Aunt Ruth said sharply, "and I also believe that you were not paying attention, Christal."

She nodded guiltily. *Please don't let her ask me why I was off in dreamland, or what I was thinking about,* she prayed quickly. Her aunt was a wonderful woman, but sometimes she could ask the most embarrassing questions at the most inopportune times.

"To catch you up with the rest of us," Papa said quickly, as if to forestall anything Aunt Ruth might say, "we were discussing the newest plans for the Winter Carnival."

"Really?" She leaned forward eagerly, completely intent on the topic at hand.

Dr. Bering chuckled. "I thought that would bring you back to us. Yes, we're talking about the latest developments. The plans for the ice palace are being finalized."

"When is it going to be built?" Mother asked. "I'm surprised they haven't started yet."

The doctor shrugged. "My understanding is that they will assemble it shortly before the carnival itself. I suppose the very nature of the bricks dictates that. What if we had a thaw and it melted?"

"That's an excellent point," Papa said.

"But there is something that I do know," Dr. Bering continued. "Christal, I was just telling your family and Isaac that the committee is planning a series of parades, including a nighttime one."

"A parade!" She clasped her hands together delightedly. "Oh, I do love parades!"

"They're going to be quite an assortment, too, so that there'll be something for everyone."

"What will there be? Will the king and queen be there?"

"I suppose they will be. Right now the fellows are working on getting sports teams lined up." Dr. Bering reached for his teacup, which was dwarfed by his huge hands.

"Sports?" Isaac shook his head. "Like baseball? In winter?"

"Not baseball. They're thinking winter sports, like tobogganing or curling."

"Winter sports," Isaac repeated.

Christal grinned. She could tell he was unconvinced about the concept of winter games. "You don't sound as if you quite accept the notion of tobogganing or curling as a sport."

He tilted his head to the side, as if considering her words. "I don't know if it's so much that as it is that the term *winter sports* seems to be impossible."

"Oh, pshaw!" Aunt Ruth tapped her cane on the floor. "People can have an enjoyable time, with good clean fun, any time of the year. So it's snowing. Or not. What does it matter?"

"Now, Ruth," Dr. Bering admonished gently, "Isaac is new to St. Paul. He hasn't had the chance to learn everything about being up here, such as how people who live in cold climates manage to have sporting events year round."

"I certainly hope I'm not giving you all the impression that I'm opposed to anything having to do with cold or snow or winter," Isaac said. "Trust me, I am not. I'm going to be attempting to enjoy it all, even though it may be quite alien to a southern soul like myself. I'm afraid that I'm coming across as being cranky, and I'm not."

"We understand," Papa said. "This is quite a change for you in many ways, and climate is a major one. But I suspect you'll be fine. Say, Isaac, have you ever been to a curling tournament?"

Curling was one sport that Christal had never been able to appreciate, although her father enjoyed it. Still, it was fascinating to watch, even if she couldn't appreciate the subtleties of it.

"No," he said, "I've never seen it, but I know what it is. It's a Scottish sport, I understand, in which the players slide a handled stone down a sheet of ice, and they do all kinds of things to keep it going where it needs to go."

"That's an excellent description," Dr. Bering said.

"That's all I know," Isaac confessed. "Last Sunday some fellows at church commandeered me to try to get me interested, but they failed."

"Curling's very popular here," Papa said, "so at some point you'll undoubtedly find yourself at a bonspiel, which is what they call their competitions."

"As a spectator, not a participant," Isaac responded, his eyes twinkling golden in the lamplight.

"As all of us in this room are," Mother agreed.

"Excuse me," Dr. Bering said, hooking his thumbs under his suspenders. "I will have you all know that I was once on a curling team."

Aunt Ruth jabbed him with her cane. "You must not lie, Alfred."

"I'm not lying. It's the truth. A patient of mine was with one of the local clubs, and he invited me to give it a try. So I did."

"How did you like it?" Christal asked.

"I think I slid down the ice better than the stone did. It's amazing how quickly an overweight man can zip across a sheet of ice."

"Well, then, maybe you have a talent for it," she said.

"I don't think so. Apparently I wasn't supposed to cross the ice on my stomach, and you know, it's odd, but they never invited me back."

They all laughed, and Dr. Bering said, "I have so enjoyed my time here tonight, but my nephew and I must return to our own home and to sleep. Another day of keeping St. Paulites in good health awaits us both tomorrow."

At the door, Isaac hung back near Christal. "How's the cooking going?" he whispered.

"I've graduated from burning my hair to cutting my finger." She held up her bandaged forefinger.

"Ah," he said, and before she could react, he lifted the injured finger to his lips and kissed it. "The best medicine in the world."

With that, he turned and left.

And Christal knew she was in love.

❧

The morning air was icy, and Isaac tiptoed to his slippers, trying to avoid too much skin contact with the cold floorboards.

He'd stayed up much too late reading. His uncle had started him on the habit of reading for leisure in the evening, and Christal had shown him the delights of the St. Paul Library, where he'd found a collection of short stories by Mr. Nathaniel Hawthorne that had turned out to be riveting.

He shivered as he got ready for the day ahead.

In one of his early classes he'd been taught that heat rises. If that was true, why on earth was his bedroom so incredibly chilly? He hurried into his clothes, anxious to get downstairs where the fireplace would already be stoked back into life and the rooms filled with heat.

He could smell breakfast. His uncle was a firm believer in the necessity of a big breakfast. Already, Isaac thought, as he had to yank on his trouser button at his waist, he was starting to fill out a bit too much with all this food.

Bacon, eggs, sausage, toast, and coffee—he could identify them all as he loped down the stairs.

"You know," he said to his uncle as he entered the kitchen and sat at the table, "I think a man could have breakfast for every meal and be quite happy."

Uncle Alfred poured him a cup of coffee and handed him the pitcher of cream. "I believe you're right. I suppose we start the day with the best so we can face what's ahead in good spirits."

He sat across from Isaac and said his usual, "Shall we?"

It was his signal that the time had come to say grace.

When Isaac was growing up, the grace had been a simple rhyme, said with habit and yet supported by belief. He'd never much thought about the words they'd used—*Bless the food for our good. Guide our day in Your way*—but subtly they had touched him.

His uncle, however, never used the same prayer twice. Each day it was different.

They both bowed their heads, and Uncle Alfred said the grace. "Today, dearest Lord, we will meet the sick who need Your healing touch. We will meet those in need who crave Your blessings. We will meet our friends in whom we see You. Keep us always mindful of You. May we be Your hands, Your feet, Your heart. Sanctify this food we are about to eat so that it may serve us as we serve You. We ask it in Your name. Amen."

Isaac raised his head and, as he reached for the platter of bacon, asked his uncle, "Did you ever consider the ministry? You are a powerful pray-er, as they say."

Uncle Alfred took a bite of sausage, chewed, and swallowed, and then answered. "I guess you could say that my doctoring is my ministry. We teach by what we live, you know. I'm known as a devout Christian, and perhaps my example has given strength to those who have needed it the most."

"Like John Lawrence?"

"Ah, John." His uncle spread jam across a piece of toast. "John is a good man. His faith teaches me. It's pure and strong."

"He's a widower, isn't he? Did you know him then?"

Uncle Alfred nodded. "I did. I was just starting out in my practice, and I knew the woman he married actually better than I knew him at the time. We had been in school together. You know, there was quite an age difference between him and his wife. She was so young, which made it all that much sadder—if one can even measure one death sadder than another."

"I suppose his faith held him up then."

"No."

Isaac nearly dropped his fork. "No?"

"He was a mess when she died. He blamed God. He said that if God had been fair and just, He would have taken some criminal rather than her. Someone who didn't deserve to live. That either God had made a mistake or God was cruel."

"That seems rather. . .harsh."

"It seems rather honest, I'd say."

Isaac stared at his uncle. "What? How can you say that? That's terrible!" He knew he was sputtering, but he couldn't stop himself.

His uncle's large hands reached across the table and gripped Isaac's forearms. "Listen to me. This may be the most important thing you learn for a long time. Grief has its own voice. It's loud and practically shouts in your ear. It demands to be heard, and it must have its say."

"But to utter those things—" Isaac couldn't imagine it.

"Again, it's the voice of grief. God knows all about it."

"But now John is a stalwart Christian, isn't he?"

"He is."

"How did he work his way through it? How did he answer those questions?"

Uncle Alfred shrugged. "He came to his own peace with it. He struggled his way from the depths, and he climbed to the heights. I don't know what the resolution was, just that there was one. The rest is between the man and his God."

It made sense. "You're telling me to respect that, aren't you?"

His uncle smiled. "I am. The relationship between you and God is not the same as mine is with Him. We need to accept that and keep it front and center as we treat those who come to see us. Remember they're not just patients. They're people who are patients. People who are children of God."

"I see."

"And speaking of children of God, our first patient is Mrs. Bonds, who is about to present us with one of those children. I'm recommending to Matthew Everett that the church select her and her husband as their Christmas family—I refuse to call them a project—since they could use a little boost right now."

"What will this mean to her?" Isaac asked, finishing up the last strip of bacon.

"There will be food, of course, and clothing and bedding for the baby. I'm going to request that the church also take up an offering for them to help with whatever else they might need," his uncle said as he stood and began to clear the table.

"Don't they get any presents?"

His uncle stopped suddenly. "You're right! Presents! Isaac, you're brilliant!"

"I am?"

"Yes, you are. We've been thinking about what they need in terms of things, day-to-day things, and we should have been thinking about the things that make life brighter and better. I like that. I'll make sure that happens. Like a necklace for Mrs. Bonds, and for Mr. Bonds, what?"

Isaac shook his head. "I don't know. I've never met him."

"Give it some consideration, and let me know what you come up with."

They washed up the breakfast dishes, each deep in his own thoughts, and when at last they'd dried the last cup and hung the towels, they looked at each other with anticipation.

"Got anything?" Isaac asked.

Uncle Alfred swung his head back and forth. "Nope."

"We'll keep thinking on it then."

"We will," his uncle said as they left the kitchen. Then he stopped and slapped his hand on his forehead. "Well, of course! I've got the perfect solution! We'll ask Ruth. She'll know exactly what to do."

"Humph," Isaac said with a grin. "She'll buy them both jackets."

seven

Christmas flew in on the snowflakes—snowflakes that melted as fast as they fell. After a dive into temperatures that were well below zero, the thermometer rose just as rapidly as it had fallen, and the holiday was unseasonably warm.

"Isaac must truly think we are crazy to live here," Christal said to her mother as they prepared the Christmas dinner. "A seventy degree temperature hike in a matter of days!"

"He's bound to be happy now," Mother agreed. "Say, look at these pies. See how the crust is a nice golden color? You want to watch them closely and take them out just as they turn this shade. Any longer in the oven and the crust will be dry and tough."

Christal beamed at the pies. Her contribution had been to roll out the crusts under her mother's watchful eye. What had seemed so simple had ended up taking nearly an hour. First, the dough stuck alternately to the rolling pin and the board. Then it was too long and narrow to fit the pan, so she had to start all over. And twice it broke apart as it was being moved to the pan.

This wasn't the first time she'd tried to make pies, but today she'd persevered and hadn't abandoned the project and given it over to her mother to finish. That alone made her immeasurably pleased.

They were beautiful pies, even if the undercrust was patched together with a watered forefinger. The pumpkin pie's crust was crimped almost evenly. Christal had misjudged the circumference and the size of her thumb a little bit, so where the end met the beginning there was a bit of a clump. The apple pie's elegant *A*, carved on the top crust by her mother's artful hand, hid a great crack that appeared as Christal carefully laid the dough atop the filling.

"Pies are awfully hard to make at first," her mother told her, "but you've been marvelously patient, and I commend you."

The turkey was roasting itself, as Mother explained it. "The less you peek at it, the better. Let the steam build up in the oven to keep it tender and juicy. Every time you open the door, you release some of that moisture, so avoid it if you can."

Christal was surprised at how easily she was able to do more in the kitchen. She accomplished more and more of the tasks and had become comfortable with her mother's recipes that had challenged her—and defeated her—before.

Aunt Ruth had, for this meal's preparations, sat in the parlor with Papa, knitting and listening as he read aloud.

Christal beamed with pride as she called them in to dinner. The table was spread with a linen tablecloth, and they were using the best china.

In the middle of the table was the turkey, gloriously golden.

They sat together and held hands in a circle, and Papa said grace. "Bless us on this holy day, the day in which a new life began so long ago, and which begins in us anew. Today, and every day, may we know the spirit of Christmas in our hearts, the joyous excitement of life ahead. In Your holy name, we pray."

The dinner was wonderful, every single crumb and flake and slice of it.

The only improvement could have been the addition of the two bachelors next door, but as usual, Dr. Bering had insisted that he—and now Isaac—celebrate the holiday privately.

Afterward, they gathered in the parlor, where usually each person selected their favorite occupation. Christal read, her aunt knitted, her mother embroidered, and her father slept.

This time, when she had finished cleaning the kitchen and joined the others in the parlor, she sensed something was different. The knitting was laid aside, as was the embroidery, and her father was wide-awake.

"Christal, dear, please sit." Her mother's voice was surprisingly nervous.

She slipped into her usual seat, but she couldn't slouch down into it as she often did. Something was going on.

"Today when I said the grace, I mentioned *the joyous excitement of life ahead*," her father said. "Do you remember that?"

She nodded, although the truth was that she had been so excited about the dinner she'd only listened to the prayer with half her mind.

Papa reached out and took her mother's hand. "We have an announcement to make." Her father paused. "This is something we've prayed about. We are planning to embark on an adventure. We're going to be missionaries!"

"We are?" Missionaries! She tried to take it all in. Her mother's face was creased with concern, and Christal stood to go to her side and give her a hug—although who she was reassuring, her mother or herself, she could not say.

"No, *we* are. *You* aren't." Her father's voice was subdued.

She stopped. "I'm not? I'm not going with you?"

"Christal, you can't go with us. We are considering a seven-year commitment." Mother reached out for her, but Christal stepped away.

"I could go."

"You can't."

"If you wanted me to go, I could go. You don't want me to come with you!" The pain was so intense that the tears refused to fall. Her head felt like it would burst.

"It's not that, honey." Her mother shot a despairing look at her father. "We're going to a place that is so distant, so undeveloped, that you'd be miserable. There aren't libraries, no schools. The buildings are minimal, and we'd be building the only church. Plus, your health—"

"I want to go." A volcano of anger rose within her. "I am no longer sick. Will you never see that?"

She had never spoken to her parents like that, but they had never proposed anything quite as life shattering as this.

"Christal, no." Her father's words were quiet but firm.

Aunt Ruth stirred in her chair, and Christal spun around to look at her.

"What about Aunt Ruth? You're leaving her, too? Oh!" She sat down as she realized what the plan would be. "I see. Aunt Ruth and I will stay here." She smiled at her aunt.

Her parents shook their heads. "No," they said in unison.

"What about her then?" she cried. "Is *she* going with you?"

"I'm also going to be traveling," Aunt Ruth said, "but not with them."

"You're going by yourself?" This made no sense to her.

"No." Aunt Ruth touched her upswept hair self-consciously and sat a bit straighter.

"Then what?"

"I," Aunt Ruth said with a faint smile, "am going to be traveling with Alfred. We are getting married in April, and he and I will head off to Miami, where we'll get on a ship and head to Borneo and Egypt and Argentina, living the vagabond life."

"You and Dr. Bering? You're getting married? So, are you in love?" she blurted out.

Her aunt blushed, a charmingly youthful reaction. "Don't be impertinent, Christal Maria Everett."

"So, Mother and Papa, if you go to Bora-Bora or wherever, and Aunt Ruth goes to Cairo, where do I go?" She buried her face in her hands.

"Your father and I won't go until next fall at the very earliest," Mother said, getting out of her chair and coming to kneel at Christal's chair. She ran her hand over her daughter's hair. "We won't leave until you're settled."

"I will," said Aunt Ruth, bluntly. "No matter what, I've got a date to become Mrs. Alfred Bering on April 27, 1886, and then I'm on a train to Miami and then on a ship, destination: Borneo!"

Merry Christmas to me, Christal thought. *Merry Christmas, indeed!*

◆

"I think the Bonds family liked their gifts," Isaac said to his uncle as they retired to the chairs near the fireplace after their Christmas dinner. They had delivered the baskets of presents to the expectant couple before sitting down to their own meal.

"The idea of the book for Mr. Bonds was truly inspired. *Around the World in Eighty Days* by Mr. Jules Verne was an excellent choice."

"That's the book you gave me, you might remember." Isaac smiled. "I took it only because you're my uncle and I have the greatest respect for you, but I knew I wouldn't enjoy it. I was incredibly wrong."

"I'm glad you enjoyed it."

"I did. I've been reading every evening, mainly shorter

works, but earlier this week I went to the library and borrowed *Twenty Thousand Leagues under the Sea* by him, too. I thought I'd start it today as a Christmas gift to myself."

"I like that idea. A good book on Christmas Day— excellent. I'm sure Mr. Bonds is sitting with the book open now. Didn't you think that Mrs. Bonds seemed to genuinely like the necklace Ruth selected for her?"

"She did. She put it right on. Did you notice that Ruth included scarves, hats, and mittens for both of them? She knitted them herself, along with a blanket and little socks for the baby." Isaac grinned. "If she'd had more time, she probably would have knitted them all jackets, too."

"True!"

"Well, they seemed to enjoy the day, even if the baby didn't make a Christmas appearance."

Uncle Alfred looked at the anniversary clock on the mantel. "It's not even seven o'clock yet. There are still five good hours left in the day."

"I am so stuffed," Isaac commented as he leaned back and sighed contentedly, "that I'm afraid she'd have to have that baby here. I don't think I could walk to our front door, let alone to her house. Do you think she could let herself in? And we could just tell her from our chairs what to do?"

His uncle chuckled and slid down into the chair, putting his feet up on the ottoman and undoing his collar button. "I don't think so. I'd never tell a woman in labor what to do. I let her tell me what to do. The body knows."

"I wonder if Christal and her family will come over tonight," Isaac said.

There was a pause before his uncle answered. "I don't think so."

"Why?"

"Well, it's Christmas."

"No." Isaac considered sitting up but decided that sprawling was easier. "I mean why the hesitation? What did you mean by that?"

"What did I mean when I didn't say something?"

"Yes. No. Oh, I don't know." The fire was warm and the food was settling so nicely that he wanted to just drift off to sleep.

"I suspect they're trying to calm Christal down. She's probably really upset." His uncle's voice was very soft, so soft that at first Isaac wasn't sure he'd heard it correctly—or at all.

"Upset?" Isaac struggled upright. "Why would Christal be upset?"

Uncle Alfred pulled himself to a sitting position. "Matthew and Sarah are leaving next fall to be missionaries, and in the spring Ruth and I are getting married and traveling the world."

This was not the kind of announcement one should try to assimilate when one had eaten entirely too much Christmas dinner, Isaac thought. One should be awake and alert and smart, not sleepy and lethargic and dull.

Missionaries? Married? Traveling the world?

The meaning began to sink in.

"Christal, too?" Christal was leaving? Moving away?

Another angle of the situation struck him, and the stupor began to wear off rapidly. "If you go, that means—"

His uncle nodded. "It does. You have to be ready to take over."

"How soon?"

"April 27th, eleven o'clock. That's the time that Ruth walks down that aisle and I officially retire from doctoring and start living my life with the woman I love."

"That's only four months away."

"Four months, one day, and sixteen hours, if my math still holds."

"I thought you said you'd be here for two years." Isaac swallowed, trying to force down the lump of fear that seemed to have grown in his throat.

"I will be, off and on. But for the most part, you'll be the doctor."

"I won't be ready! I can't—"

"You can, and you will. You have the knowledge and the book training. Now all you need is to fine-tune it with some understanding of how people get ill, and as importantly, how they recover."

He shook his head vehemently. "I can't—"

"I'll be coming back regularly—in between trips to far-off climes with my love, where we'll wear tropical flowers around our necks and play drums in the sand and get sunburned in January. And besides, I'm not leaving tomorrow."

Could he do it? Could he learn all he needed to know in that short amount of time?

And what about Christal? What would she do? Would she stay in St. Paul?

What would he do if she didn't? What would he do?

He was a doctor—or almost one. He knew that the human heart was an organ, the same as a liver or a lung. It beat, in a generally regular pattern, from before birth and quit only when life on earth was done. Its job was to pump blood through the body's circulatory system.

That was all it did. It couldn't break. It couldn't feel emotions. Hearts weren't sorry or sad or devastated. Their owners were.

Like him.

Yet his heart was aching already. He couldn't lose her. He

couldn't. Somehow he'd find a way to keep her here. He had to!

"She's not going with them," Uncle Alfred said from the depths of his chair. Isaac realized that his uncle had been studying him.

"She isn't?" His question came out in a high-pitched squeak, and he cleared his throat.

"No. Matthew and Sarah are going by themselves."

"So," he said, slowly, trying not to sound as excited as he felt, "Christal will be staying here?"

"That I couldn't tell you. I suppose that's Christal's decision."

"What would she do here? Would she have to find employment? Where would she live? Next door?"

His uncle shrugged. "I know the house belongs to the church, so I'd say that she couldn't live there unless she stayed on as a maid or a cook."

A maid or a cook? Christal?

"I suppose she could find work at the library here. She'd be a marvelous employee," Uncle Alfred mused. "She knows the books inside and out."

"Where would she live? In a boardinghouse?"

"That, or as a roomer somewhere."

He'd known her only two months, but he knew that she wouldn't be happy in either situation.

"They'll figure it out," Uncle Alfred said. "After all, Matthew and Sarah won't be leaving until early autumn. There's plenty of time. Plenty of time. Not to worry."

His uncle's voice trailed off as he drifted to sleep.

But Isaac was wide-awake. *Not to worry?* How could he not worry? He was worried about Christal, but he was also very concerned about himself. Was he ready to take over as a full-fledged doctor within a few months?

He put his hands together, palm to palm, and bent his

head over so that his fingertips touched his brow.

When things seemed insurmountable, there was only one path. He took it. He began to pray.

It wasn't one of the beautiful prayers that came from his uncle's lips or the clear ones that he heard from Rev. Everett's pulpit each Sunday. It was a wordless mishmash of concerns, of cares, of wants, of needs, all laid at the table of Heaven. Soon it began to sift through, until he was left with one unavoidable fact.

He was in love with Christal, and he couldn't live without her. They belonged together. Perhaps, perhaps—he couldn't go further with the unspoken thought this early on, but it took up residence in his soul and settled in for a long stay.

His heart, that insensate organ he'd been mulling about earlier, did an odd little leap. It felt like joy.

≈

Christal retired to her room as soon as she could. She wanted to take her aching head away from her parents and aunt, who were trying very hard to make her feel better—and failing miserably.

They all had plans. They all had something exciting and different to look forward to, but she didn't. She had nothing but a big open abyss.

They all assured her that they were not abandoning her. Her mother repeated that she wouldn't leave until Christal had a home and a source of income, but neither she nor Christal's father had any suggestions about that. She wasn't trained to teach. She'd make a miserable cook or maid. Perhaps she could find a job at the library. She could ask tomorrow.

They didn't understand that her distress wasn't just about not living in this house where she'd spent her entire life, or having to find employment in a world that didn't offer much to women. From now on she would be alone. For the next seven years, unless she opted to spend Christmas with her parents in their missionary home, they'd be apart for the holidays.

This would be the last time they celebrated Jesus' birth together.

Or at least the last time for a long time, she added as a hasty amendment to her stream of thought. She'd have a family, but they'd be gone.

Even Dr. Bering. It struck her like a bolt of lightning. Even Dr. Bering!

And if Dr. Bering left, would Isaac stay?

If he left, too—she couldn't bear it. She just couldn't.

A man shouted outside, and she raced to her window. Isaac stepped out of Dr. Bering's carriage.

The door of the house opened, and two men emerged—Dr. Bering and a man she didn't recognize but who looked terrified. His hat was askew, and his jacket flapped open in the night chill.

Isaac looked up at her window and waved at her, but his face was solemn.

Something was going on.

She hadn't changed into her nightclothes yet, so she ran down the stairs, threw her jacket on—ignoring her aunt's pleas to button it—and sped to the carriage.

"Is everyone all right?" she asked breathlessly.

"My wife's having a baby!" the man she didn't recognize said.

"This is Mr. Bonds. Mr. Bonds, Christal Everett." Dr. Bering put his hand on the fellow's back. "My good man, let's get in the carriage and see about putting that baby into your arms as soon as possible."

Isaac was behind them, and she could see the anxiety on his face. "You'll be all right," she whispered, patting his arm.

"It's my first baby," he answered with a tight smile as he began to climb into the carriage. "I've never delivered a baby before. And this one is a Christmas baby. They say doctors never forget their first delivery."

"It'll be fine. Just fine. Go on now. I'll be praying."

He stopped midstep and smiled. "Thank you."

"Come on, Isaac! Babies wait for no one!" his uncle called from inside the carriage, and Isaac got behind the horses, pulling his doctor's bag inside with him, and picked up the reins.

The carriage clattered away, and Christal watched it, her heart riding with it.

❧

The woman twisted in the bed, the blankets tangled around her arms and legs. Her face was dotted with sweat, and her husband stood at her side, wringing his hands together fiercely.

Isaac knew that labor was painful, but it was one thing to read about it on paper and another to see it in its vivid reality.

"Can't you help her?" Mr. Bonds asked, his voice hoarse with fear. "I know you wanted us to go to the hospital, but it was Christmas, you know, and we thought we'd spend this time alone, and the pains came faster and faster. . ."

"That's all right," Uncle Alfred said soothingly. "Women have been having babies in homes for hundreds and thousands of years. This baby will be just fine being born here."

The room was small and dark and lit only faintly with a single lamp. They hadn't covered this in medical school— delivering a baby in a room that was the size of a closet.

Nor had they told him what to do when he had to work with only the instruments in his doctor's bag. He hoped that if all went well, the only item he'd need would be the scissors to cut the cord.

The hospital would have been better. Now that those in medicine realized how much safer a hospital birth was, more women were using maternity hospitals. There was a new one in St. Paul, and his uncle was enthusiastic about it. But this baby was going to be born at home, not in the controlled surroundings of the hospital.

His uncle sat beside the woman on the bed. "Hello, Mrs. Bonds. It's almost time for you to see your child!"

She moaned in response, the sheets clutched in her white-knuckled grip.

"Can't you stop the pain?" her husband asked. "Make it stop? I can't bear to watch her like this."

His voice was tense with unshed tears, and Uncle Alfred patted the worried man's hands. "The only thing that will make this stop will be the appearance of Baby Bonds. Are you ready to become a father tonight?"

"Yes." The man looked again at his wife and wiped the sweat from her forehead.

"Good. Now, Mr. Bonds—"

"Jeremy. Please call me Jeremy."

"Very well. Jeremy, you could be a great help if you'd gather some things for me. Some boiling water, and some chilled water. Some ammonia. A bar of soap, too, would help. And some cloths, please, preferably ones we can discard at the end of this."

"Why would we want to—" the husband began, and then he stopped. "Oh. Oh!"

He turned and slipped out of the room, his fingers still working wildly together.

"Why do we need ammonia?" Isaac asked.

"We don't. We needed him out of the room."

His uncle turned his attention to the woman on the bed. "Mrs. Bonds, I hope you don't mind my bringing in my nephew. Is it all right if he stays?"

She nodded. "This. Hurts. So. Much."

"I have heard that," Uncle Alfred said soothingly. "But the reward at the end is great."

"I have never had pain this bad in my entire life," Mrs. Bonds said, reaching out and gripping Isaac's hand so tightly that his knuckles cracked in protest. "This is—" She screamed as a contraction seized her.

"Your body is helping the baby come out," Uncle Alfred said. "It's all going as it should. Do you have a name for this child yet?"

"David if it's a boy, and Elizabeth if it's a girl." The woman panted and then tensed as another contraction took over. "How soon? How much longer?"

Uncle Alfred did a quick and discreet examination and smiled. "I think we're due for a baby very soon here. Go ahead and scream if you want, or—"

Her husband reentered the room. "I heard her scream again. That was right after the other one. She's—"

"She's having a baby, and we're getting closer." Uncle Alfred reached for a cloth and dipped it in the cool water and wiped it across her forehead and over her cheeks. "Go ahead and try to let your body have this baby. Don't fight the pain; it'll make it worse. Breathe, Mrs. Bonds. Breathe. In and out. That's right. If you do that during the contraction, it'll be better."

Her husband stood at the side. "I feel so helpless. I want to help her, and I can't. I don't have anything I can do to make it better. And I feel so guilty."

Isaac shot a look at his uncle. How would he deal with that?

Amazingly, his uncle laughed. "As well you might. But trust me when I tell you that in a very short time, this whole experience will be overshadowed by something that will amaze you beyond anything else. In just a few minutes—"

"Something, something, something is happening! Oh, it is!" Mrs. Bonds curled and straightened. "I think I'm—"

"Isaac, I think it's time. Are you ready? Let's deliver this baby!"

Uncle Alfred lifted the blanket, the woman screamed one more time, and Isaac helped a wet, wriggly baby into the world.

The baby was beautiful, perfect in every way. He handed the baby to his uncle, who wiped it with a cloth, checking it over as he did so

"Congratulations! You two are the parents of a perfect baby boy. David, right?" Uncle Alfred laid the baby on Mrs. Bonds's chest and reached out as Isaac handed him the scissors. "Isaac, would you like to tie the cord?"

He couldn't make his hands stop shaking as he reached over and tied the cord on the baby, whose screams took over where his mother's left off.

His first birth. There was nothing as incredible as what he'd just seen.

"There's one more thing I always do when I deliver a baby," his uncle said.

"What's that?" Isaac looked around. What was left?

"I always offer thanks and ask the Lord's blessing."

"Please do," Mrs. Bonds said softly, her lips pressed against her baby's forehead.

The four of them encircled the newborn child, united in

prayer. "Thank you, dearest Lord, for this gift of life, the ultimate gift of Christmas. Bless David through his years ahead, and guide his feet to walk in Your service, his hands to share Your abundance, and his lips to sing Your praises. In the name of all that is holy on this day of Christmas, amen."

"Amen." Isaac breathed. "Amen."

eight

"It was incredible!" Isaac enthused as they walked home from church together. Two weeks had passed since the birth of the Bonds baby, and he was still talking about it.

Christal tried to feel happy for him, but her own situation kept her outlook bleak. Her future was dim and dark and foreboding. At least that was the way it seemed.

She'd gone to the library to ask if she might find employment there, but the librarian had shaken his head. No jobs.

Her hands were jammed into her pockets and her scarf wound tightly around her neck, and she burrowed into the wool as if hiding from the world.

Her mood wasn't just about her. More than anything, she wanted her parents to be happy, and that would mean that they would go on this missionary sojourn. She could tell from their voices that it was important to them.

"So I think that I can do it. I'm really feeling energized. Maybe it's the new year; maybe it's that new baby. I don't know, but I'm happy!" Isaac threw his arms out wide, nearly knocking Christal into a leafless shrub. "Oh, I'm sorry!"

"That's all right," she said gloomily. "If I had a branch from that chokecherry bush stuck through my chest, maybe I could say things were looking better."

He stopped, faced her, and put his hands on her shoulders. "I'm sorry. I know that you're going through some dark times now, but trust me—they'll improve. There will be a solution."

She wanted to believe him, but his words were just the flat

142

meaningless syllables she heard from her own family. *Trust.* Her ability to trust was being tested.

"What am I going to do? What?" She knew she was being fretful, but she couldn't help herself.

"Something will come along."

"It won't."

"Oh, Christal."

Suddenly his arms were around her, and his lips grazed the thin area of exposed skin between her eyebrows and the bottom brim of her knit hat.

She was so bundled up that she had no sense of where her body was, and there was just a bit of ice on the sidewalk. The next thing she knew, she and Isaac were tumbling down onto the ground.

Her hat had slid entirely down over her face, and her scarf was caught on the buttons of his overcoat.

Something scratched her neck under her coat collar, and she realized that they were at the base of the chokecherry and one of the branches was digging into her skin.

"I shouldn't have said anything about being impaled by the bush, because I am—" she said as she struggled to an upright position, tugging her hat back up. "Oh!"

His face was just inches from hers, his arms around her waist, and he grinned. "And I shouldn't have tried to kiss you."

Suddenly brave, she smiled. "I'm glad you did."

"I should do it again."

"Perhaps."

He bridged the short gap between them, and his lips touched hers.

The branch scratched more sharply at her neck, but she ignored it. He was kissing her, and for the moment the cares of her life fell away. Locked in his embrace, there was no one but the two of them, nothing but this kiss.

He pulled away. "I think this is not the place, sprawled here on the street, although I have to say I would happily stay here, frozen in your arms."

"We'd be the talk of the church, then, wouldn't we?" She unhooked her scarf from the front of his overcoat. "And we'd probably be famous. I can see the headline on the *Dispatch* now: 'MINISTER'S DAUGHTER GOES TO HEAVENLY REWARD WHILE SMOOCHING THE NEW DOCTOR ON THE STREET UNDER THE CHOKECHERRY BUSH.'"

"That's a long headline," Isaac said, grinning as he helped her to her feet.

"News like that doesn't come along every day here in St. Paul, you know." She dusted the snow off her elbows and what she could reach of the back of her coat.

"Well, since we're newsworthy now," he said, linking her arm in his, "I wonder if we could possibly consider going into full courting now?"

"Courting?" She swallowed hard. More than anything she wanted to look at him, but her head seemed locked into place, and her ability to speak was stifled. He was asking permission to court her! She had dreamed of this, hoped for this, wished for this; and now that the moment had arrived, she had no idea what she should say or do.

"Yes," he said, and she could hear the amusement behind the single word.

"I, well, yes, I suppose, we, I imagine, um, why not?"

"Not the most fervent avowal of interest that I've heard," he said, "but I'll take it."

She looked at him at last and saw again how kind he was. How happy he was. How gentle he was.

"How's this?" she said. "I would be delighted to be courted

by you, Mr. Almost-Doctor Bering."

"Better. Much better. I'd kiss you again, but the neighbors would definitely be talking."

"They're already talking."

"Very well."

He leaned over and kissed her again, a proper and sedate kiss, yet warm in the brisk January air. She wanted to linger, but she knew they were already late for dinner.

He took her mittened hand in his as they walked the last steps to their block. He stayed with her, as he always did, until she arrived at the door of her house.

"Would you do me the favor of accompanying me to the Winter Carnival parade?" he asked.

"My, aren't we formal!"

"We're courting. That's the way it's done—I think. I've never courted a woman before."

"And I've never been courted." The heat climbing her cheeks told her she was blushing, but she didn't care.

"See? We're perfect for each other."

"Indeed."

"So will you?"

"Will I what?"

"Go to the Winter Carnival parade with me?"

"Yes, I will."

"Because we're courting?"

"Because we're courting."

He kissed the tip of her nose, winked, and left, taking her heart with him.

❧

Sometimes, Isaac thought, in the bleakest of moments, God showed Himself the clearest.

His uncle had fallen asleep in the parlor, a book open on his chest, but Isaac was too excited to nap.

Was what he had done all right? Had he been too forward?

He hadn't been joking when he told her he was inexperienced with courting. He'd gone out with some young women, but nothing had been serious or lasted for long. He'd never let himself get involved with matters of the heart.

At first he'd been too immature to settle down, and he'd gone from one girl to another, enjoying each girl's company but never finding the desire to stay with any certain one. Then as he got older, his studies came first. He rarely left his room once classes were over for the day.

Now, as the inevitability of his future weighed in on him, he realized that he was, indeed, going to be a doctor, and furthermore, he did not want to be alone.

God gave Adam a helpmate in the Garden of Eden, and that had gotten the proverbial ball rolling for romance. What had always captured Isaac's interest in the story of Adam and Eve was the question: Did Adam and Eve love each other?

He thought the answer was yes, that when God created the first two, He created the first couple, and He created the first romantic love.

So Isaac had never considered that he would ever marry without a deep love. That was what God wanted. It was what Isaac wanted.

He'd known Christal only three months. He knew without a doubt that she was the one he wanted to spend the rest of his life with. But three months wasn't very long.

If her parents hadn't decided to go to a missionary post, and if his uncle hadn't decided to marry Ruth and travel around the world, things might have gone at a different pace. But those two factors moved everything along faster, and the next thing he knew, he was kissing Christal again.

The remembrance made him smile.

Kissing Christal was very nice. He hoped to do it again. And again. For the rest of his life.

It would be the answer to her problem, and to his.

He still had time to let the idea rumble around in his head for a while. Her parents wouldn't leave for eight months at the earliest. His uncle had said that his wedding to Ruth was scheduled for April. He didn't want to be hasty, though. What was that his mother used to say? *Marry in haste, repent at leisure.* He nodded slightly. It was best to be wise about this and not to rush into something he might rue later.

His uncle mumbled something in his sleep, and Isaac's attention turned to him.

Uncle Alfred was an amazing man. A skilled doctor, he'd built his talent not only on the knowledge of the human body, but as importantly, knowledge of the human soul.

He'd been single his entire life, choosing to marry only when retirement was possible. Isaac smiled as he realized that his uncle would approach marriage with the same single-mindedness, making it the center of his world, assigning it the utmost importance.

A thought struck him. His uncle had clearly separated the two, being a doctor and being a husband. Did he think it wasn't possible to be both at the same time?

He frowned as he considered that. He would be starting out as a new doctor. Maybe the time was wrong to be courting anyone. A medical practice would take almost all of his energy, especially when he was following in the footsteps of someone as beloved as his uncle.

His uncle stirred again, and Isaac studied his face. Uncle Alfred's main diversion was reading, which he believed helped him in his doctoring. One of their earliest conversations, about the Jules Verne book, returned to him, and he could hear in his memory his uncle's words about how even science fiction helped him understand his patients.

But might it also be that such reading provided a very needed respite?

"Is something written on my face?" his uncle asked, startling Isaac so sharply that he jumped.

"You startled me."

Uncle Alfred sat up, his round face wreathed in good humor. "You've been staring at me so long that I was beginning to wonder if I had a story on there."

"No," Isaac answered. "I was just thinking."

"If you would like to talk, I would like to listen."

"I was thinking about love."

"Ah! An excellent topic."

Isaac mustered up all his courage. "Why did you never marry?"

His uncle smiled. "What do you think?"

"I don't know. That's why I was thinking."

"You're a smart young man. When you don't know something, you think. That is excellent. Too many people, when they don't know something, do just the opposite. They stop thinking."

Isaac tilted his head, his gaze steadily on his uncle. "Was it because you felt you couldn't practice medicine well and be married?"

Uncle Alfred chuckled. "There are plenty of doctors who are married, and they're fine physicians. No, Isaac, I didn't get married because I quite simply found no one who captured my heart to the extent that's necessary to have a successful marriage."

"But Ruth—oh!" Isaac leaned forward and lowered his voice. "Were you in love with her when she was married to her husband?"

"No," his uncle answered, "there's nothing as intriguing as that. The simple answer is this: Over the past year or so, Ruth and I've come to spend more time together, and we've found that we share many things, not the least of which is our faith in God. That smooths the way quite a bit."

He laid his book, which had been spread open across his chest, on the table beside him. "The more time I spent with her, the more I liked her, and that turned into deep respect and then love. In our case, love was the ripe fruit on the vine."

Isaac sighed. That was just the opposite of what he felt for Christal, which were the first eager buds, not the "ripe fruit" his uncle referred to.

His uncle put his head back and closed his eyes again. "Christal is a charming young woman. You are an intelligent young man, and I love both of you as if you were my own. But I'll tell you this."

He shifted in his chair. "One day you will grow old. You'll have wrinkles, and you won't be able to remember the name of your cousin in Baton Rouge, and she'll have aches and pains, and her hearing will fade. That's when you get to see the miracle of love. It does something to the eyes. She'll still be as beautiful as she is today. It does something to the memory. Old slights vanish into the mists of the past. It does something to the fingers. They gnarl and don't feel the roughness the years have wrought on the other's hand."

He didn't speak again, and Isaac thought his uncle had gone to sleep. Then, at last, he spoke once more.

"Marry her."

❧

Excitement along the parade route was almost palpable. Talk of the carnival was everywhere—in church, in the shops, along the streets—and now that the opening was only two weeks away, hardly anyone spoke of anything else.

Plus, if there was one thing that the residents of St. Paul liked, it was a parade, and the organizers had scheduled them regularly until the first day of February, when the carnival began.

"This is the first parade of many before the carnival starts, my father told me this week," Christal said. "But I think it's going to be the biggest, except for the one on opening day, of course."

"It seems as if everybody in the city is here," Isaac commented.

It certainly looked liked it. The street was solidly lined with people who were anxious to see what the first parade of the season would be like.

"My parents are here," she said, craning her neck to see if she could find them, but there were so many people, she'd never locate them. "And I think Aunt Ruth and Dr. Bering are here, too."

"Oh, my uncle is, most definitely. He's very excited about this. I can't imagine that he'd miss it." He grinned at her. "He left before me, and he was wearing a heavy jacket, buttoned up, and a muffler and a big fur hat and thick mittens, so I'm guessing that Ruth is with him."

Christal laughed. "They'll be on some tropical isle, and she'll make him button up his sarong so he doesn't catch a chill."

"Sarongs have buttons?" The corners of his eyes crinkled with amusement.

"They will when Aunt Ruth finishes with them."

Standing there with Isaac, waiting for the parade to start, made the uncertainty of her future seem far off, nothing that she needed to worry about at the moment. Right now, her whole focus was the parade and Isaac and how wonderful she felt.

"Don't you think parades are the best thing ever?" she asked, wrapping her gloved hand around his arm.

"I've never been to a parade."

"What? How can that be?"

He turned to her and shrugged. "A parade just never came my way, I guess."

"You can't wait for a parade to come to you. You have to go to the parade."

She couldn't imagine never having seen a parade. In St. Paul they were fairly regular things, celebrating all kinds of events and people and companies, and she'd attended almost every one of them.

"I love parades, especially when the band comes by, marching together and playing at the same time. If I were in it, I'd probably tromp right into the fellow next to me. I don't see how they can do both and not topple all over each other." She shook her head.

The crowd shouted, and Christal leaned forward as far as she could, with Isaac holding on to her so she didn't fall.

The parade had started.

Leading the way was the police department, dressed warmly in their winter uniforms. They strode confidently, handsome and strong with their navy blue coats with brass buttons. Two of them were members of the church, and Christal waved at them.

Then came the parade marshal and his troupe. "He looks so proud," she said to Isaac, "doesn't he?"

"He looks cold," he said with a laugh. "But he's probably got a lot to be pleased with. He—"

The arrival of the Great Western Railroad band cut off whatever Isaac was about to say. Christal clapped along with the songs as they played their way down the street. The music filled the winter day with melodies and marches.

"Oh, look at her!" Christal said as the band passed them and a sleigh with Clemence Finch in it drew near. "She's the carnival queen, and the daughter of George Finch, the organizer."

Clemence Finch was beautiful as she waved at the people along the street. Her curls glowed like burnished gold under her hat, and her short red coat was bright in the sunshine.

"I've heard she's wearing the Nushka toboggan team's jacket," Isaac said.

Christal sighed. She knew she shouldn't be envious—it was a sin—but it must be so much fun to wear a jacket like that and ride in a sleigh in a parade and be the carnival queen. Some things, though, were simply out of the reach of a minister's daughter.

After the sleigh came the governor, the mayor, and other dignitaries, looking stiff and formal in their long coats. Yet under the stately top hats, Christal noticed, the men all beamed happily.

Then came the sports clubs. Snowshoe clubs, toboggan clubs, and ski clubs—they all celebrated winter with great gusto. One club, the Ice Bears, brought shotguns that they fired every few minutes into the air. Christal kept a watchful eye on them and held her hands over her ears as they walked past. It didn't seem safe at all, but no one else appeared to worry.

A huge sleigh, shaped like a ship, followed the clubs. Finally, the firemen, postmen, military men, and members of the horseshoe and curling clubs ended the parade.

Christal sighed happily. Here she was watching a parade with Isaac, the man who was courting her.

"What did you think of your first parade?" Christal asked him.

"It was amazing," Isaac said.

"Wasn't it?" Her mind was filled with the images and sounds from the parade. "I wouldn't have changed a thing."

"I would."

"What would you have changed?" she asked in astonishment.

He pretended to shiver. "I'd have had it indoors!"

nine

The days until the carnival were filled with parades and great speculation about the ice palace. Christal had heard murmurs about what it was going to be like, but none of it seemed to be at all possible. The construction was finally beginning, but the majority of it would be done quickly, right before the start of the carnival.

"An ice-skating rink?" Isaac said one evening as they sat in the parlor eating his uncle's gingerbread. Now that they were officially courting, the older family members left them alone more, although Christal had seen some inquisitive faces peeking around door frames throughout their evenings together.

"Maybe it's a very small ice-skating rink." Christal took a bite of the gingerbread.

"You mean the size of one that might be in someone's yard?" he asked.

"One summer when I was nine, one of my friends and I decided that we would make a wading pool behind our house. We dug and dug, and finally we had a fairly respectable hole."

"Your parents were supportive of it?"

"I'm not sure they understood the scope of our plan," she admitted. "Remember, this is me, the same person who had a pet toad. Anyway, we decided the pond needed fish, so we went down to the river, and after getting our clothes snagged on dead trees and our feet ripped up on rocks, we managed to capture a couple of little fish."

He leaned back, smiling as he listened.

"We got back to the house and realized that we had a bit of a problem. The water we'd put in our pool, all painstakingly carried bucket by bucket from the well, had run out. There was nothing there but a mud hole."

"That doesn't sound good," he commented.

"It wasn't. My parents got upset when they saw what a mess we'd created. They made us take the fish back to the river and let them go, and we tried to fill in the hole, but mud has a mind of its own. No matter how hard we tried, we couldn't get the ground level again."

"Especially if you're only nine years old."

"Exactly. Plus every time it rained, it got worse. It never dried out the rest of the summer. That winter, though, we had a wonderful area for ice-skating back there, so it wasn't a total loss."

"So you think that the ice-skating rink at the ice palace is going to be the same thing?" he asked.

"I think it'll be planned a bit better," she said, laughing.

Her father cleared his throat from the doorway. "We've had just about enough of hiding out in the kitchen. It's time for us to go home, Christal."

She popped the last of the gingerbread into her mouth. "Waste not, want not. But I'll still want more later on."

"Dr. Bering gave your mother a platter of it," Papa said, "so I think you'll live through the night. Isaac, you're going to the opening of the ice palace?"

"Christal and I are going to it as soon as the last patients leave. You know that I was a doubter all along, but I've been impressed so far with what I've heard and seen of the Winter Carnival. Tomorrow will be the pinnacle. First, though, we'll go to the last parade of the carnival. I hear it's going to be quite a spectacle."

"I've been told the same thing. Christal, shall we?"

As they proceeded to the entryway, Christal hung back to walk beside Isaac. Their fingertips brushed and intertwined.

Courting, she thought, was really quite wonderful.

"I'll see you tomorrow," he said at the door. "Finally, the carnival!"

As soon as she got home, she said good night to her family and went to her room. She had to be alone with her thoughts.

Had her life ever been such an odd mixture?

She was in love, and yet mixed in with her great happiness was great sadness.

Within eight—no, seven!—months she would be on her own. A huge wall of loneliness loomed ahead of her. What would she do without her parents and her aunt? And Dr. Bering?

She probably could, if she fought hard enough, go with her parents on their missionary trip, but even as she considered the idea, she dismissed it. The reason was simple: If she were with her parents, she wouldn't be with Isaac.

She wanted them all to stay together, for everything to remain exactly as it was now. That would be perfect.

"Perfectly unrealistic," she said in disgust.

No, what was going to happen was going to happen, and she needed to acknowledge that.

Or she could not think about it at all. At least not tonight. Maybe after the carnival, when the world got bleak again, she would deal with it. Right now, though, life in St. Paul was exciting and vivid, and she was going to enjoy it.

She pulled a book off her shelf and plumped up the pillows on the bed before plopping down to read. It was a European legend in a collection of stories she had borrowed from the library, and in it there were a king and a queen and a prince and a princess and a palace. Within moments she had left frozen Minnesota and was on the French countryside, astride a white steed.

In this story, no one left the princess, and they all lived happily ever after.

She got to the end of the book, closed it, and clasped it to her chest. "God," she said softly, "do fairy tales ever come true? Or is that why they're called 'tales,' because they don't?"

❧

"And so, we're off to the last parade of the carnival!" Isaac announced to his uncle. "I have to say I've become quite a fan of these events, but I am looking forward to viewing one in the summer! Are you ready? I'll go next door and—"

Ruth Everett burst in. "I'm sorry for not knocking, but it's John. Come quickly. I'll get Sarah, and we'll meet you there."

Isaac and his uncle looked at each other, and each seized his medical bag and threw on jackets and sped out the door, racing to John Lawrence's house.

The man was on his chair, his eyes shut. Aristotle flew from one corner of the room to the other, cawing with great agitation.

Uncle Alfred dropped to his knees beside Mr. Lawrence and put his fingers aside the sick man's throat. "His pulse is thready but there. Help me."

They lifted Mr. Lawrence and carried him to the couch where they stretched him out. Isaac straightened the sick man's arms and legs and rubbed them, trying to generate blood flow.

Uncle Alfred raised Mr. Lawrence's torso, placing pillows under his chest and head. He then covered his extremities with a light blanket. "Let's make it as easy for him as possible. He'll breathe more comfortably if he's on an incline, but you're right to massage his extremities."

With his stethoscope, Isaac checked the patient's heartbeat and respiration. "I don't know," he said to his uncle. "Would you listen?"

The older doctor did, and rocking back on heels, he said, "The congestion is thick."

"What do you think?" Isaac asked, afraid to hear the answer.

His uncle only shook his head.

Ruth came in with Mrs. Everett. "We'll be in the kitchen if you need anything. Tea? Coffee?"

"Tea would be good, thank you." Uncle Alfred's voice was calm, and Isaac was reminded of what one of his professors had said, warning them about upsetting the patient with their tone of voice. *Stay calm*, the professor had said, *to keep the patient calm.*

John Lawrence's breathing became labored, with longer periods between each inhalation. Isaac leaned over and again placed his stethoscope against the man's chest. The rattle was unmistakable. Isaac had read about it, the death rattle, but this was the first time he'd heard it.

Without a word, Uncle Alfred lifted the blanket that covered the man's feet. The skin was mottled, nearly blue and white. He met Isaac's eyes and rewrapped the man's feet.

"Lord of all we know, this is Your blessed servant, John Lawrence. He has been Your own from his first breath, and now as he undertakes his last journey to Your arms, we ask that You hold him tightly in Your arms. Cradle him now as You did when he came to us at his birth."

The man coughed a bit, and Uncle Alfred wiped his lips and swabbed his mouth with water.

Isaac took the old man's hand in his own. It was cold, an indication that Mr. Lawrence was nearing his final moments on earth. His eyes filled with tears. How could he let this man go, after all he had done to try to pull him through? How did his uncle do this, praying the patient into heaven? He knew that Mr. Lawrence was old, and that there wasn't anything they could have done to save him from death. Yet it didn't soften the loss. He barely knew Mr. Lawrence, but in the short time he had known him, he'd taken him to his heart because of the older man's gentle ways and true faith. Isaac truly believed that this man was going into heaven, that he was stepping upwards as the culmination of a life of faith, but how was he to manage? What was he supposed to do?

Uncle Alfred wiped the man's face again and hydrated his lips. "You've had a good life, John," he said, "and I know that you are bound for Glory. You—"

The man lifted his head, and his face broke into a beaming smile. "Maryanne!" he said in a long exhalation. He held the posture, and time stood still until at last he smiled even more widely and dropped back upon the pillow.

Uncle Alfred ran his fingers over the man's face and looked at Isaac. "It's all right to cry."

Isaac realized that his face was wet, and he put his head in the palms of his hands. Sob after sob wracked his body as he sat at the bedside.

His uncle stood and made his way around the bed to put his hands on Isaac's shoulders. "This seems like a loss, but it's a win. He's going to heaven. I know that. You know that."

Isaac reached out and touched Mr. Lawrence's face. So this was what death looked like. It looked quite a bit like life, as if he were still breathing.

"Uncle Alfred!" he shouted. "Uncle Alfred! He's not dead!"

"No," John Lawrence mumbled. "Not dead." He took a deep breath, coughed, and breathed again.

His uncle laughed and rubbed the wizened hands of the elderly man. "You old codger! I thought you'd gone to your heavenly reward!"

Mr. Lawrence opened his eyes a slit and smiled slightly.

"Do you know that you went right to that door of heaven, my friend? I suspect you even peeked in between the posts, just to see." Uncle Alfred laughed again. "I think you'll have many more days with us."

Ruth and Mrs. Everett rushed in from the kitchen. "What is all the noise about?"

Aristotle resumed his frantic flights across the room, squawking at the women.

"God wasn't quite ready for our friend." Uncle Alfred turned to Isaac. "Sometimes we're fooled as doctors. We think we know exactly how life is going to go, how death is going to go, and we are wrong. This is one of those instances. Remember that in all things, God is the One who is in control. He wasn't ready for John to advance to heaven. Not yet."

The crow flapped over to the couch and plucked a button off his owner's shirt.

"God looks after this crazy crow as much as He does his owner, and I guess He wasn't ready for one without the other," Ruth said with a fond smile.

"Aristotle," John Lawrence said, lifting his hand. The bird jumped onto it, bit the man's knuckle, and flew off to the top of the bookcase.

"That," said Mrs. Everett, "is love."

His uncle decided to stay a bit longer, and Christal's mother volunteered to sit with Mr. Lawrence. "You and Ruth go ahead," Mrs. Everett said. "Take Christal to the carnival."

The carnival! He'd forgotten all about it.

Ruth Everett had her hand on the door when he went to leave.

"To walk with you, Ruth Everett, I'll even button my coat and put on my hat and gloves."

Christal's aunt laughed. "You're a quick study, Isaac."

As they walked back together, she told him stories of her youth, of the good times they'd all had, ice-skating and sledding and having snowball fights.

"It was as if we were crazed to have our last moments of wildness before putting on the heavy garments of adulthood. We played, we gamboled. . ."

"You gambled?" He couldn't imagine her with a pair of dice or a deck of cards in her hand, not now, not as a young woman. "I can't see you at a game of chance, gambling."

She laughed. "Gamboled with an *o*. As in, we frolicked. We reveled. We celebrated whatever could be celebrated. And probably some things that couldn't. You know what it's like."

Actually, he didn't. Having spent his entire youth as a somber, study-absorbed child, going to college simply moved him to the next stage of the same behavior. The thought of letting himself act so freely ran contrary to the way he was.

He couldn't gambol *or* gamble.

He realized that she was watching him with a puzzled look on her face. "You didn't, did you?"

He cleared his throat. "Didn't what?"

"Didn't enjoy the carefree days of childhood."

This was wrong. He drew himself up straighter and protested, "I did. I had a wonderful childhood."

"Oh, Isaac, I didn't mean that!" Her hand flew up to her neck and fluttered around the knot of the scarf like a wizened sparrow. Her face was wrinkled with concern. "I know your family was wonderful. Alfred has spoken often of the kindness of your mother and the love your father shared with his children."

"I was a somber child, and I am a somber adult," he said. "It just simply is not in my nature to be merry and convivial."

She stood on the street, studying him with her head cocked to one side, until at last she said, "Well, we will have to change that."

He felt himself sagging inside. He wasn't the center of attention at social gatherings; in fact, he was rarely at social gatherings. The most he could manage was church, and he shuddered as he recalled the first service he attended when he'd had to meet everyone. He'd made it through that situation only through the literal grace of God—and a certain scripture. The fact was that he didn't like wrestling with God. It was so much easier to stand firm on what was comfortable for him, to assert that this was, after all, the way God had made him and the way God had established the world around him.

He'd been ridiculously pleased, though, when he'd forced himself to greet the people at the church. To tell the truth, it wasn't as if he'd had any choice. Once Christal's father had announced his presence and invited them all to say hello to him, he'd had little opportunity to slide out unnoticed.

"Everybody needs to savor the gifts we've been given," Ruth said. "Even if we're just sitting in the sunshine or enjoying the grace of snowflakes floating to earth, we need to acknowledge and appreciate the wonders."

"I don't have time—" he began, but she interrupted him.

"Even a moment is enough. Understanding that simple beauty is really not simple at all is important. It comes from our Creator. Think, Isaac, if you had made a daisy, a little common daisy, wouldn't you be incredibly pleased? And wouldn't it be nice if someone said, 'Good job, Isaac'?"

They had come to the front of the Everett household, and he paused at the brick walkway. "I see your point," he said.

"Good. A little honest recognition of how complex the smallest part of our world is will make you truly awed."

Awed. That was exactly how he felt. Awed by the littlest detail, like a snowflake, all the way to the greatest thing, like John Lawrence's near-death.

Awed by the creations of the Lord and the creations of man. Like the ice palace.

And parades. He thought of Christal's words: "You can't wait for a parade to come to you. You have to go to the parade." It was time for him to go to the parade, in more ways than one.

❧

They missed the parade, but knowing that John Lawrence would live was worth it.

The sun was nearly set, and the sky was a vision of splendid oranges and purples and golds, like marbled fire, and the ice palace glittered in the late afternoon light. Visitors streamed toward it, drawn by the icy glory. It dominated most of Central Park with its wintry splendor.

Christal's steps slowed as she tried to take in the beauty of it. Her eyes didn't seem to be big enough to absorb it.

"It's incredible." She breathed at last.

Isaac took her mittened hand in his. "I've been reading about this in the newspaper and hearing people talk about it, but I didn't quite grasp what it was going to be like."

"How could anyone imagine something like this? It shimmers, doesn't it?"

"I know the statistics of it," he said, reaching in his pocket with his free hand. "I have it right here."

She tore her attention from the ice palace to look at him. "You have statistics in your pocket?"

"It was in the newspaper. I thought it would be interesting."

Had she hurt his feelings? She squeezed his fingers through their mittens. "It will be interesting. I was just teasing. Read on, please!"

"I won't read the entire thing, but here's the gist of it. The palace is built from twenty thousand blocks of ice, and the ice has been brought in from all around the area, even from Fargo, North Dakota."

"Why would they do that?" She turned back to study the ice castle, which shone with an iridescent gleam in the last vestiges of the afternoon sun.

He shook his head. "They needed the ice, I suppose, but I'd imagine that the folks in these other communities might have enjoyed being part of this."

"It's really much bigger than I'd ever dreamed it would be."

"According to the article, it's 189 feet long and 160 feet high. The central tower alone is 106 feet tall!"

The ice castle, silhouetted against the vermilion and scarlet sunset, was commanding. It glowed with the vivid reflected colors of the sun's last blaze, combined with the cool blues and purples and greens from within the ice itself.

"It's a frozen rainbow," she said, squeezing his hand tightly. "I've never seen anything like it."

She turned to look up at him. He was staring at the ice castle, his mouth open a bit, and his breath came out in short white puffs. He was no longer hunkered down inside his coat and muffler. Perhaps the scene in front of him was enough to make him forget how cold he was.

The last vestiges of light vanished beneath the horizon as the sun sank with its usual wintry suddenness, and Isaac sighed. "One of the oddest things about this area," he said, "is how quickly the sun sets. It lays out the most glorious palette, and then, just like that, it's done. Day is over and night begins."

"That's only in winter. In summer the sun takes a more leisurely stroll ending its daylight time, and the sunsets last longer. You'll see."

He looked at her and smiled. "I'm looking forward to that—and not just because it'll be warmer then!"

The ice palace suddenly began to glow from within, sending a kaleidoscope of color across the snow.

"Electric lights," he said to her. "There are electric lights in there. I have to see that!"

"I saw them at an exhibition last year. The fellow who was speaking claimed that there's no flame involved. It was quite amazing."

"It's the future, according to Uncle Alfred. One day that's how we'll be lighting our houses!"

She shook her head. How could anyone believe that? Light without a flame? Was it possible? And in their houses?

He tucked her arm closer to his body, and together they walked toward the palace. Around them a crowd of people surged forward, all of them headed in the same direction.

The evening was wrapped in magic. The palace seemed to be illuminated with its own radiance, still echoing the last moments of the sun's wild blaze.

" 'He casteth forth his ice like morsels: who can stand before his cold?'" she said softly.

She leaned against Isaac, taking advantage of the fur surrounding the hood of her coat to steal covert glances at him. His cheeks, above the swath of the muffler he'd wound around his neck, were reddened with the cold, and his nose was scarlet.

He wore a great fur hat that made her smile; it looked for all the world as if an oversized squirrel were perched upon his head. The poor man was dressed as if he were going on an Arctic expedition instead of just across the city.

Yet the ice palace had apparently made him temporarily, at least, forget his constant chilliness. He didn't walk bent over, as if he were trying to preserve every particle of heat possible. Instead, he stood straight and craned his neck out of the safety of the muffler to see the spectacle before him.

The crowd gave them no choice but to keep moving toward the arched entrance to the ice castle. A young woman dressed in a long white wool coat rimmed with white fur stood next to a portly gentleman in a dress overcoat. The buttons of his coat strained over his stomach, and he moved from foot to foot to keep warm, like Aristotle on his perch, Christal thought.

"Good evening!" the woman sang out. "Welcome to the Winter Carnival!"

She looked like the spirit of winter, garbed in pure white, her cheeks rosy in the cold, and she smiled widely at each person who entered the castle through the arch, motioning them in with a wave of her white-gloved hand.

The man, however, was clearly the gatekeeper, and pleasantries were at a minimum. "Twenty-five cents entry a head," he said mechanically. "Twenty-five cents."

Isaac held out two quarters, and coin and paper exchanged hands. "We've got our tickets," he said to her. "We can go in."

The young lady swept her hand toward the entrance. "Enjoy the ice palace!"

The castle was extraordinary from the outside, but inside it was stupendous. No matter where Christal looked, there was something unexpected, something wonderful.

A village of Sioux Indians was set up in one of the rooms. It was an entire encampment, and Christal's eyes couldn't stop looking at all of the details, from the tepee to the clothing. It was an astonishing display.

"They brought this all here and set it up? It looks so real!"

"It is real," Isaac said. "All of this is real."

Through the translucent walls of ice blocks, she could see people moving about. Everyone was clad in layers, and she wished she'd thought to bring her muff. Her fingertips were beginning to get numb even through the woolen mittens, but her whole arms could freeze and she wouldn't leave.

"There's the ice-skating rink," Isaac said, pointing.

"Papa told me that there are two ice-skating rinks, and a curling rink, too!" She shook her head. How could all this be? "Toboggan slides, too! I've never seen such a thing!"

"Look," Isaac said, pulling her in a different direction. "There are warming rooms! We can even buy food here!"

Christal couldn't take it all in. It was splendid beyond belief, right down to the crystalline walls and ceiling made of ice.

"It's so beautiful," she said.

Everywhere they turned, there was something else to see, each thing more amazing than the other. The dark of the night was chased away by the electric lights that punctuated the grand building, brightening every corner.

"Next week they're adding the items from the Adolphus Washington Greely Arctic expedition," Isaac said. "His sled will be here, and his journal, and even his gloves and his boots."

They strolled through the palace arm in arm.

She stopped suddenly and took off her mitten.

"What are you doing?" he asked in surprise.

She pressed her fingertips to a nearby wall, pulling them back only when the cold became too much to bear.

"Why did you do that?" he asked.

"It's like a dream. I had to make sure it's real."

"It's real," he said. "I'm thunderstruck—although that's probably not the right word to use in an ice palace. Whoever thought of this is a genius."

"A genius? So you've changed your mind? It's not as silly as you thought?"

"I was wrong." He laughed. "Those words don't come easily to me, understand, but they're true. This is beyond belief. It's like something from one of those fairy tales you like."

She shook her head. "Fairy tales have ogres and trolls in them."

He faced her and took her hands in his. "Let's make this a real fairy tale, Christal. This is a castle, and you're a princess. That much is true. Would you consider letting this very common man spend his life with you?"

Her breath caught in her throat. "You mean—?"

"In simple English, please marry me. I love you beyond all thought. Please, Christal, marry me."

The magic of the ice palace wrapped them in a glittering embrace.

"Yes," she said. "Yes."

epilogue

From the church bulletin:

The congregation of Redeemer Church bids a fond farewell to Rev. Matthew Everett and his wife, Sarah, who have gone to Tahiti in the missionary service. As his last official act as minister of this church, Rev. Everett joined in holy matrimony his daughter, Christal Maria, and Dr. Isaac Tobias Bering.

A belated wish for Ruth and Alfred Bering, whom we have known and loved for many years, as they start the next chapter of their lives as husband and wife: May you always know sunshine.

It is written in the Bible: The greatest of these is LOVE. *And so it is.*

Dr. Bering's Spice Cookies

2 ½ cups flour
1 teaspoon baking powder
½ teaspoon baking soda
¼ teaspoon salt
1 ½ teaspoons ground ginger
1 teaspoon cloves
1 teaspoon nutmeg
¾ teaspoon cinnamon
1 cup brown sugar
1 cup shortening
¼ cup molasses
1 egg
Extra sugar (about ½ cup) to roll the cookie dough in

Mix together dry ingredients and then add shortening, molasses, and egg. Shape dough into balls about 1 to 1¼ inches in diameter, and roll in extra sugar. Place on cookie sheet, tapping each cookie very slightly to flatten dough balls a bit, and bake at 350 degrees for eight minutes. Let cookies cool on cookie sheet. Makes about 40 cookies.

A Letter To Our Readers

Dear Reader:

In order that we might better contribute to your reading
enjoyment, we would appreciate your taking a few minutes
to respond to the following questions. We welcome your
comments and read each form and letter we receive. When
completed, please return to the following:

Fiction Editor
Heartsong Presents
PO Box 719
Uhrichsville, Ohio 44683

1. Did you enjoy reading *The Ice Carnival* by Janet Spaeth?
   ❏ Very much! I would like to see more books by this author!
   ❏ Moderately. I would have enjoyed it more if

   _____

   _____

   _____

2. Are you a member of **Heartsong Presents**? ❏ Yes ❏ No
   If no, where did you purchase this book? _____

   _____

3. How would you rate, on a scale from 1 (poor) to 5 (superior),
   the cover design? _____

4. On a scale from 1 (poor) to 10 (superior), please rate the
   following elements.

   _____ Heroine   _____ Plot
   _____ Hero   _____ Inspirational theme
   _____ Setting   _____ Secondary characters

5. These characters were special because? _____

_____

_____

6. How has this book inspired your life? _____

_____

_____

7. What settings would you like to see covered in future
   Heartsong Presents books? _____

_____

_____

8. What are some inspirational themes you would like to see
   treated in future books? _____

_____

_____

9. Would you be interested in reading other **Heartsong
   Presents** titles? ❏ Yes   ❏ No

10. Please check your age range:
    ❏ Under 18   ❏ 18-24
    ❏ 25-34   ❏ 35-45
    ❏ 46-55   ❏ Over 55

Name _____

Occupation _____

Address _____

City, State, Zip _____

E-mail _____

SALT LAKE DREAMS

3 stories in 1

Intrigue and romance await three women in historic Utah.

Historical, paperback, 352 pages, 5¾₆" x 8"

Please send me ____ copies of *Salt Lake Dreams*. I am enclosing $7.99 for each. (Please add $4.00 to cover postage and handling per order. OH add 7% tax. If outside the U.S. please call 740-922-7280 for shipping charges.)

Name _____

Address _____

City, State, Zip _____

To place a credit card order, call 1-740-922-7280.
Send to: Heartsong Presents Readers' Service, PO Box 721, Uhrichsville, OH 44683

Presents

__HP795	*A Treasure Reborn*, P. Griffin
__HP796	*The Captain's Wife*, M. Davis
__HP799	*Sandhill Dreams*, C. C. Putman
__HP800	*Return to Love*, S. P. Davis
__HP803	*Quills and Promises*, A. Miller
__HP804	*Reckless Rogue*, M. Davis
__HP807	*The Greatest Find*, P. W. Dooly
__HP808	*The Long Road Home*, R. Druten
__HP811	*A New Joy*, S.P. Davis
__HP812	*Everlasting Promise*, R.K. Cecil
__HP815	*A Treasure Regained*, P. Griffin
__HP816	*Wild at Heart*, V. McDonough
__HP819	*Captive Dreams*, C. C. Putman
__HP820	*Carousel Dreams*, P. W. Dooly
__HP823	*Deceptive Promises*, A. Miller
__HP824	*Alias, Mary Smith*, R. Druten
__HP827	*Abiding Peace*, S.P. Davis
__HP828	*A Season for Grace*, T. Bateman
__HP831	*Outlaw Heart*, V. McDonough
__HP832	*Charity's Heart*, R. K. Cecil
__HP835	*A Treasure Revealed*, P. Griffin
__HP836	*A Love for Keeps*, J. L. Barton
__HP839	*Out of the Ashes*, R. Druten
__HP840	*The Petticoat Doctor*, P. W. Dooly
__HP843	*Copper and Candles*, A. Stockton
__HP844	*Aloha Love*, Y. Lehman
__HP847	*A Girl Like That*, F. Devine
__HP848	*Remembrance*, J. Spaeth
__HP851	*Straight for the Heart*, V. McDonough
__HP852	*A Love All Her Own*, J. L. Barton
__HP855	*Beacon of Love*, D. Franklin
__HP856	*A Promise Kept*, C. C. Putman
__HP859	*The Master's Match*, T. H. Murray
__HP860	*Under the Tulip Poplar*, D. Ashley & A. McCarver
__HP863	*All that Glitters*, L. Sowell
__HP864	*Picture Bride*, Y. Lehman
__HP867	*Hearts and Harvest*, A. Stockton
__HP868	*A Love to Cherish*, J. L. Barton
__HP871	*Once a Thief*, F. Devine
__HP872	*Kind-Hearted Woman*, J. Spaeth
__HP875	*The Bartered Bride*, E. Vetsch
__HP876	*A Promise Born*, C.C. Putman
__HP877	*A Still, Small Voice*, K. O'Brien
__HP878	*Opie's Challenge*, T. Fowler
__HP879	*A Bouquet for Iris*, D. Ashley & A. McCarver
__HP880	*The Glassblower*, L.A. Eakes
__HP883	*Patterns and Progress*, A. Stockton
__HP884	*Love From Ashes*, Y. Lehman
__HP887	*The Marriage Masquerade*, E. Vetsch
__HP888	*In Search of a Memory*, P. Griffin
__HP891	*Sugar and Spice*, F. Devine
__HP892	*The Mockingbird's Call*, D. Ashley and A. McCarver

Great Inspirational Romance at a Great Price!

Heartsong Presents books are inspirational romances in
contemporary and historical settings, designed to give you an
enjoyable, spirit-lifting reading experience. You can choose
wonderfully written titles from some of today's best authors like
Wanda E. Brunstetter, Mary Connealy, Susan Page Davis,
Cathy Marie Hake, Joyce Livingston, and many others.

When ordering quantities less than twelve, above titles are $2.97 each.
Not all titles may be available at time of order.

HEARTSONG
PRESENTS

If you love Christian romance…

$10.⁹⁹

You'll love Heartsong Presents' inspiring and faith-filled romances by today's very best Christian authors…Wanda E. Brunstetter, Mary Connealy, Susan Page Davis, Cathy Marie Hake, and Joyce Livingston, to mention a few!

When you join Heartsong Presents, you'll enjoy four brand-new, mass-market, 176-page books—two contemporary and two historical—that will build you up in your faith when you discover God's role in every relationship you read about!

Mass Market 176 Pages

Imagine…four new romances every four weeks—with men and women like you who long to meet the one God has chosen as the love of their lives…all for the low price of $10.99 postpaid.

To join, simply visit www.heartsong presents.com or complete the coupon below and mail it to the address provided.

✂------------------------------

YES! Sign me up for Heart♥ng!

NEW MEMBERSHIPS WILL BE SHIPPED IMMEDIATELY! Send no money now. We'll bill you only $10.99 postpaid with your first shipment of four books. Or for faster action, call 1-740-922-7280.

NAME _____

ADDRESS_____

CITY_____ STATE _____ ZIP _____

MAIL TO: HEARTSONG PRESENTS, P.O. Box 721, Uhrichsville, Ohio 44683 or sign up at WWW.HEARTSONGPRESENTS.COM